Praise for *Europeana*

"Touching on subjects and events as disparate as the invention of the bra, Barbie dolls, Scientology, eugenics, the Internet, war, genocide and concentration camps, it unspools in a relentless monotone that becomes unexpectedly engaging, even frightening."—*New York Times Book Review*

"A tragicomic prose poem to make poets weep with envy, to make everyone weep."—*The Village Voice*

"The narrating voice is funny, scientific, infantile, sarcastic, and eerie . . . Europeana is a both a very strange work of history and an ingenious work of art."—*Chicago Review*

"You out there drop everything you are doing and go immediately and read this book. It's only 132 pages—reading without stopping—without breathing—you will have encountered a fantastic writer."—Raymond Federman, author of *Double or Nothing*

"Europeana is a convincing sum of that ugly century. Certainly recommended."—*Complete Review*

"Juxtaposing East and West and blurring Barbie and Buchenwald, Ourednik's stream of historical consciousness shreds familiar narrative trajectories and compresses 100 years of still-fresh history into a roughly equivalent number of pages."—*Booklist*

Other Books by Patrik Ouředník

Case Closed

The Opportune Moment, 1855: A Novel

The End of the World Might Not Have Taken Place

Deep Vellum | Dalkey Archive Press
3000 Commerce Street, Dallas, Texas 75226

www.dalkeyarchive.com

Support for this publication has been provided in part by grants from
the National Endowment for the Arts, the Texas Commission on the
Arts, the City of Dallas Office of Arts and Culture, the Communities
Foundation of Texas, the Addy Foundation, and the Ministry of
Culture of the Czech Republic.

Paperback: 9781628975017
Ebook: 9781628975253
Library of Congress Cataloging-in-Publication Data:
Names: Ouředník, Patrik, 1957- author.
Turner, Gerald, translator.

Classification: LCC D424.0813 2005 / DDC 940.5 2004063475
LC record available at https://lccn.loc.gov/2004063475
Cover design by Justin Childress
Interior design by Anuj Mathur
Printed in Canada

Patrik Ouředník

EUROPEANA

A BRIEF HISTORY OF THE
TWENTIETH CENTURY

Translated from the Czech by Gerald Turner

DALKEY ARCHIVE PRESS
Dallas, TX / Rochester, NY

EUROPEANA

THE Americans who fell in Normandy in 1944 were tall men measuring 173 centimeters on average, and if they were laid head to foot they would measure 38 kilometers. The Germans were tall too, while the tallest of all were the Senegalese fusiliers in the First World War who measured 176 centimeters, and so they were sent into battle on the front lines in order to scare the Germans. It was said of the First World War that people in it fell like seeds and the Russian Communists later calculated how much fertilizer a square kilometer of corpses would yield and how much they would save on expensive foreign fertilizers if they used the corpses of traitors and criminals instead of manure. And the English invented the tank and the Germans invented gas, which was known as yperite because the Germans first used it near the town of Ypres, although apparently that was not true, and it was also called mustard because it stung the nose like Dijon mustard, and that was apparently true, and some soldiers who returned home after the war did not want to eat Dijon mustard again. The First World War was known as an imperialist war because the Germans felt that other countries were prejudiced against them and did not want to let them become a world power and fulfill some historical mission. And most people

THE ENGLISH INVENTED THE TANK

in Europe, Germany, Austria, France, Serbia, Bulgaria, etc., believed it to be a necessary and just war which would bring peace to the world. And many people believed that the war would revive those virtues that the modern industrial world had forced into the background, such as love of one's country, courage, and self-sacrifice. And poor people looked forward to riding in a train and country folk looked forward to seeing big cities and phoning the district post office to dictate a telegram to their wives, I'M FINE, HOPE YOU ARE TOO. The generals looked forward to being in the newspapers, and people from national minorities were pleased that they would be sharing the war with people who spoke without an accent and that MARCHING they would be singing marching songs and jolly popular ditties SONGS with them. And everyone thought they'd be home in time for the grape harvest or at least by Christmas.

Some historians subsequently said that the twentieth century actually started in 1914, when war broke out, because it was the first war in history in which so many countries took part, in which so many people died and in which airships and airplanes flew and bombarded the rear and towns and civilians, and submarines sunk ships and artillery could lob shells ten GERMANS or twelve kilometers. And the Germans invented gas and the INVENTED GAS English invented tanks and scientists discovered isotopes and the general theory of relativity, according to which nothing was metaphysical, but relative. And when the Senegalese fusiliers first saw an airplane they thought it was a tame bird and one of the Senegalese soldiers cut a lump of flesh from a dead horse and threw it as far as he could in order to lure it away. And the soldiers wore green and camouflage uniforms because they did not want the enemy to see them, which was modern at the time because in previous wars soldiers had worn brightly-colored uniforms in order to be visible from afar. And airships and airplanes flew through the sky and the horses were terribly frightened. And writers and poets endeavored to find ways of expressing it best and in 1916 they invented Dadaism because everything seemed crazy to them. And in Russia they invented a revolution. And the soldiers wore around their neck or wrist a tag with their name and the number of their regiment to indicate who was who, and where to send a telegram of condolences, but if the explosion tore off their head or arm and the tag was lost, the military command would announce that they were unknown soldiers, and in most capital cities they instituted an eternal flame lest they be forgotten, because fire preserves the memory of something long past. And the fallen French measured 2,681 kilometers, the fallen English, 1,547 kilometers, and the fallen Germans, 3,010 kilometers, taking the average length of a corpse as 172 centimeters. And a total of 15,508 kilometers of soldiers fell worldwide. And in 1918 an influenza known as Spanish Flu spread throughout the world killing over twenty million people. Pacifists and anti-militarists subsequently said that these had also been victims of the war because the soldiers and civilian populations lived in poor conditions of hygiene, but the epidemiologists said that the disease killed more people in countries where there was no war, such as in Oceania, India, or the United States, and the Anarchists said that it was a good thing because the world was corrupt and heading for destruction.

WORLD
HEADING FOR
DESTRUCTION

But other historians said that the twentieth century actually started earlier, that it began with the industrial revolution that disrupted the traditional world and that all this was the fault of locomotives and steamships. And yet others said that the twentieth century began when it was discovered that people come from apes and some people said they were less related to apes because they had developed more quickly. Then people started comparing languages and speculating about who had the most advanced language and who had moved furthest along the path of civilization. The majority thought it was the French because all sorts of interesting things happened in France and the French knew how to converse and used conjunctives and the pluperfect conditional and smiled at women seductively and women danced the can-can and painters invented impressions. But the Germans said that genuine civilization had to be simple and close to the people and that they had invented Romanticism and lots of German poets had written about love, and about the valleys where there lay mists. The Germans said they were the natural upholders of European civilization because they knew how to make war and carry on trade, and also to organize convivial entertainments. And they said the French were vain and the English were haughty and the Slavs did not have a proper language and language is the soul of a nation and Slavs did not need any nation or state because it would only confuse them. And the Slavs, on the other hand, said that it was not true, that in fact their language was the oldest of all, and they could prove it. And the Germans called the French WORM EATERS and the French called the Germans CABBAGE HEADS. And the Russians said that the whole of Europe was decadent and that the Catholics and Protestants had completely ruined Europe and they proposed to throw the Turks out of Constantinople and then annex Europe to Russia so as to preserve the faith.

The First World War was also called a trench war because after a few months the front became static and the soldiers hid in muddy trenches and at night or at dawn they launched

PATH OF
CIVILIZATION

EUROPE WAS
DECADENT

offensives intended to capture twenty, thirty or fifty meters of enemy territory. And they wore green and camouflage uniforms and bombarded and shot at each other. The Germans had mine-throwers and the French had mortars, so they could lob shells at each other. When some detachment launched an offensive the soldiers had to jump over other trenches and cut barbed wire and avoid mines and the enemy fired machine guns at them. And the soldiers would spend entire months and years in those trenches and they were bored and frightened and played cards and gave the trenches and passages various names. The French devised names like THE SNAIL, PLACE DE L'OPERA, BAD LUCK, THE DESERTER, ILL FEELINGS, and HEADACHE, while the Germans chose names like GRETCHEN, BRUNHILDE, BIG BERTHA, and BLACK PUDDING. The Germans said the French were vain while the French said the Germans were uncivilized. And they no longer believed that they would be home for Christmas and they felt abandoned and unloved. News came from the military headquarters that the war was nearing its end and melancholy was to be avoided, spirits were to be kept up and patience and a positive attitude were required, and in 1917 an Italian soldier wrote in a letter to his sister I FEEL THAT EVERYTHING THAT WAS GOOD WITHIN ME IS GRADUALLY LEAVING ME AND I FEEL MORE AND MORE CERTAIN EVERY DAY. And it was a great medical mystery that plague did not break out in those trenches because rats lived with the soldiers and ate the corpses and bit the fingers and toes of the living. In the military headquarters they feared that a plague would break out and it would allow the enemy to capture defensive positions, and so a reward was offered for every rat killed, and the soldiers shot at the rats and cut off their tails as evidence and in the evening they delivered them to a special commissary for rats' tails, who counted them and said how much each had earned but the payment never came because no fund had been created. Lice also lived with the soldiers. Sometimes when the

SOLDIERS LAY IN WAIT

soldiers lay in wait for the enemy at night they would hear an enemy soldier scratching himself and it told them where he was and they would fire in that direction and hurl hand grenades. But there were still as many lice and enemies.

In the twentieth century there was a swing away from traditional religion, because when people discovered they came from apes and that they could travel by train and talk by telephone and go down in a submarine, they started to turn away from religion and attend church less and less and they said that there was no such thing as God and that religion kept people in ignorance and in the dark and that they were for pos-

POSITIVISM

itivism. Positivism was a philosophical doctrine that declared that human judgment and the understanding of phenomena were the results of natural and social sciences and the only truth was what was scientifically verifiable and metaphysics was nonsense. Positivists did not believe in any God, although initially some said that some higher being could exist and that it was scientifically feasible although it could not be proved. But scientists said that life was solely the result of chance and

ORDER AROSE OUT OF CHAOS

that order arose out of chaos, and they did not believe in the creation of the world as it was supposed to have happened six thousand years ago according to Christian tradition. And astrophysicists said that everything was only a matter of quarks and atoms and gases and that the universe was twelve to fifteen billion years old and that it was expanding all the time, but they did not know whether it would go on expanding or whether it would start to shrink again one day, or whether it might just blow up. Believers said that man might have come from the apes and quarks and atoms and gases but that did not alter anything because somebody must have created the apes and quarks. And it did not particularly matter whether the universe came into existence six thousand or fifteen billion years ago, because the important thing was what went before and science was no match for that. The astrophysicists said that there was nothing before then and believers said that that was precisely what was written in the Bible. As time went by, positivism lost some of its attraction because people did not know what do with progress and submarines and the atom bomb and started to wonder if they might manage to achieve some transcendence after all. And some scientists said that scientific research had no chance of disproving God and that even though science could not provide irrefutable evidence of the existence of God or some higher being, it could pave the way for a scientifically grounded answer to human questioning, namely that the meaning of life and the mind of God were actually identical. And the philosophers wondered whether God might not exist virtually, at least, although this would be an oxymoron.

EXIST
VIRTUALLY

At the end of the nineteenth century people in cities looked forward quite impatiently to the new century, because they felt that the nineteenth century had marked out the paths that mankind would travel. And in the future everyone would make telephone calls and travel by steamer and be transported by subway and ride escalators and conveyor belts and use quality coal for heating and even bathe once a week. And the electromagnetic telegraph and wireless telephony would carry human thoughts and desires at lightning speed through space and enable the human community to achieve harmony and live in peace and unity. And a great event was the Paris World Fair in 1900, which, on the threshold of the new age, extolled

THRESHOLD ⊙
THE NEW AGE

the future and the paths that mankind would take, and the visitors rode a moving sidewalk and admired the inventions and marveled at the new artistic trends. And they believed that the twentieth century would put an end to poverty and drudgery and the opportunities afforded by electricity would surpass their wildest dreams. And everyone would enjoy social security and a week's paid vacation. And people would live comfortably and hygienically and democratically and women would live democratically too and would be able to go to the polls and vote for their political representatives. And they could not wait for the twentieth century and would declare that it would mean new opportunities for mankind and we would

LEARN FROM
ST MISTAKES

have to learn from the mistakes of the past. Women started to vote in 1906 in Finland, and in 1913 in Norway and in 1915 in Denmark, etc., and as time went by they also wanted to study and sit for exams and take part in politics and science and fight in armies for a just peace. Most men did not entirely agree with women's demands and considered that women chiefly had an instinct for family life and minor jobs in the household, while men had a more developed propensity for the organization of society and abstract thinking and community life and convivial entertainments. And in some democratic countries it was laid down by law that there had to be equal numbers of men and women in parliament, but some

WOMEN ARE
UMAN BEINGS

women said that this was not democratic because women were first and foremost human beings. And it was not just if they only bore children and washed diapers, etc., and just waited for their husbands to come home with their wages. And some men said that they would sooner be at home and wash diapers, etc., and not go to work anymore, and in Sweden, where they had strong social policies, there were lots of men who were paid so that their wives could work. And according to various opinion polls, lots of people considered that the greatest event of the century was the invention of contraception, because it meant that women could have intercourse whenever they felt like it and did not have to worry about becoming pregnant, and that enabled them to achieve sexual independence and economic independence too, because they were able to apply for all sorts of important jobs, and they no longer fainted at the sight of a mouse because they had ceased to submit to male stereotypes about women. Sociologists said that the traditional model of women in Western society was now obsolete, because after submitting to the natural order for centuries, women had now joined the contractual order thanks to contraception. And they said that the emancipation of women was actually a paradox of coercive freedom because women had more and more responsibilities and duties, and those things that were formerly regarded as major social achievements and privileges of women, such as the ban on night shifts and maternity leave, etc., were now regarded by women as a form of oppression.

At the end of the twentieth century people were not certain whether they were to celebrate the beginning of the new millennium in 2000 or 2001. It was important for people who were waiting for the end of the world, but most people did not believe in the end of the world, so they did not care. Other people were waiting for the end of the world but thought it would happen on any old day. And some Christians said that in reality it was already 2004 because Jesus had been born four years earlier than was supposed. And according to the Jewish calendar it was already 5760 and according to the Muslim calendar it was only 1419 and according to the Julian calendar it was less than according to the Gregorian one, which is also why the October Revolution in 1917 did

INVENTION OF
CONTRACEPTIC

END OF THE
WORLD

not break out until November. And the Buddhists did not care either because according to the Buddhist calendar it was year 2542 and Buddhists were more interested in what they would become in the next life, a frog, a long-tailed monkey, etc. In the twentieth century, Buddhism and Taoism gained many adherents in Europe who banged gongs and breathed YIN AND YANG through their diaphragm and talked about yin and yang and wrote mystical books and said that the world was full of mysteries, but only apparently so, because in reality everything was harmonious. And when someone experienced a mystery, they wrote a book about it because the media era had arrived and everyone wanted to write a book. And people were not so worried about the end of the world as about terrorist attacks and BREAKDOWN a breakdown of electronic systems that would disable television and VCRs and microwave ovens and ATMs and airports and freeway signs and traffic lights and elevators in high rises. Terrorist attacks in the twentieth century multiplied because it was a way of showing that someone deeply disagreed with something and the most famous of all was the assassination of the Austrian archduke in Sarajevo in 1914 that caused the First World War and thereby the twentieth century too. The breakdown of electronic systems that experts warned citizens about was called the MILLENNIUM BUG and it could have occurred at midnight on December 31st, 1999 when the date changed to 1.1.00, because most computer applications used a two-figure year code and the danger was that the electronic systems would identify the year 2000 as the year 1900, as if the twentieth century and the assassination of the Austrian archduke had never happened.

During the First World War they also created wartime propaganda because the war was omnipresent, even at home, and if

it was to finish as soon as possible, people had to be prepared
for sacrifices and accept them with determination. And lots of   LOTS OF
MEN WERE
FIGHTING
men were fighting at the front and women had to work instead
of them in factories, public transport, etc. And ministries of
information devised posters addressed at the civilian population. And the Austrian women on the posters said WIR HALTEN
DURCH! and the British women on the posters said WOMEN OF
BRITAIN SAY—GO! and Hungarian women on the posters said
HA MAJD EGYSZER MINDNYAJAN VISSZAJOENNEK! and the Italian
women on the posters said SEMPRE AVANTI! and the French
women on the posters said ILS SONT BRAVES, NOS GARS! and
the American women on the posters said GEE! I WISH I WERE
A MAN! I'D JOIN THE NAVY! And the women meant, we don't
give in, forward, one day they'll come home, ever onwards,   FORWARD
our boys are fearless. Soon children started to appear on the
posters too and one English poster was a painting of an egg
out of which crept a toddler with a gun and fixed bayonet
asking ARE THERE ANY FRITZES LEFT? And at the ministries of
information they tried to think up the best ways of assisting
the final victory. And the Germans said that French ate frogs
and the Russians ate little children, and the French said that
the Germans ate little children and tripe. And women also
sent packages and letters to unknown soldiers at the front
and the soldiers would reply and ask them how old they were.
Sometimes a soldier was killed before the letter reached him
and the commander would look for someone with the same
Christian name among his troops who had not received a letter yet. Women sent letters and worked in the munitions factories, where they manufactured bombs and poison gas. In
England, a million women worked in the munitions factories
and an average of eighteen of them went blind every day and
others died of gas poisoning. The women who worked in the

munitions factories had orange hair and yellow faces and people called them canaries. And doctors estimated that two thirds of them would be barren after the war. Poison gas was used to demoralize the enemy soldiers, but the gas did not enable the enemy lines to be breached. And the soldiers who didn't manage to put on their gas masks in time behaved as if they were drowning. The ones that knew the crawl stroke acted as if they were swimming it, while those that could not do the crawl, swam breaststroke or doggy paddle. And they tried to swim out of the gas to where they might breathe.

THE ONES THAT KNEW THE CRAWL

Before the First World War, people in cities used kerosene lamps for lighting, and in the country they lit candles and used coal or wood for heating, but before long electricity started to reach the cities, thanks to which even the wildest dreams could be realized in the new century. At first, people in the countryside were frightened of electricity and did not know what it might be good for, because very few people owned a radio or gramophone. It was only after the Second World War, when they started to make refrigerators and washing machines and televisions, that people in the countryside said they would listen to the radio and watch television to find out what was going on in the cities, and they demanded that the government should install electricity for them. Engineers called radio wireless telephony, and some elderly people thought that radio was like the telephone and they had paid in advance for someone to telephone them and let them know where a war had broken out. And when they first watched television, they thought it was like the kinetoscope that they had seen at the world fair, and that someone in the building, such as a daughter-in-law or grandchild, was turning a handle and making fun of them. Some elderly people were also in the habit of replying to the

WHAT ELECTRICITY WAS GOOD FOR

questions asked by television or radio presenters, such as when someone on the television or radio said AND WHAT DO YOU THINK HAPPENED NEXT? they would say WELL, I REALLY DON'T KNOW, or when someone on television or the radio said AND WHAT DO YOU THINK THE WEATHER WILL BE LIKE TOMORROW? they would say IT'S ABOUT TIME WE HAD A DROP OF RAIN, OR IT'LL PUT AN END TO THE HARVEST. Great achievements were also scored in the field of hygiene, because before the First World War people bathed infrequently and when they did, the whole family bathed in the same tub, or the whole family and the neighbors, etc. Rich people in the cities had their own bathtub and eventually piped in hot water. But for a long time other people from the cities and the countryside were frightened of hot water because they thought there were microbes in it. They did not know for sure what microbes were, but imagined them to be something that healthy living did not require. And doctors organized information programs to inform people and explain that there were just as many microbes in cold water as in hot, although that was not entirely clear. As a result little by little people started to bathe regularly, once a month, once every two weeks or once a week, even in the countryside. And by the end of the century people in developed countries would bath or shower twice a day or even more and everyone had flush toilets and tear-off toilet paper. Tear-off toilet paper was invented by a Swiss paper manufacturer in 1901, on the same day that the Swiss government handed over to Italy an Anarchist suspected of assassinating the Italian king, and the newspapers said that it was a humble but important invention. And in 1914, a Frenchwoman invented the brassiere and the newspapers wrote that the invention of the brassiere would mean a new way of life for women who yearned for a sportier and more modern lifestyle, and that the demise of the

DOCTORS ORGANIZED PROGRAMS

INVENTION O THE BRASSIEF

laced-up bodice marked the end of the old world, which had been laced-up with all kinds of prejudices. And in 1935 the Americans invented the brassiere with padded cups for women with small breasts. And in 1968, when women in Western cities were demonstrating for women's rights, they deliberately ripped off their brassieres in front of journalists to show that rights should be the same for men and women. And water consumption per capita rose from ten liters a day to one hundred and fifteen and groundwater levels fell throughout the world and there was a danger that in fifty or one hundred years' time water would start to be in short supply.

ROUNDWATER
LEVELS FELL

In the first year or year-and-a-half of the First World War it sometimes happened that soldiers stopped firing at each other and an undeclared truce reigned for several hours, and the soldiers behaved almost as if there was no war on. At Vauquois, the Germans had a trained dog that would run back and forth between the German and English lines carrying bread and cigarettes and chocolate and cognac. The Germans had cigarettes and chocolate but did not have bread or cognac, and the English had plenty of bread and cognac but not enough cigarettes. And at Predazzo, the Austrian soldiers sent a cat to the Italians with the card bearing the words WE'RE SENDING OUT OUR CAT WITH A CIGAR. The cigar was tied to the cat's back with a piece of string. And the Italians smoked the cigar and killed and ate the cat. And at Carency on Christmas Eve in 1914 the German and French soldiers sang carols together and drank to each other's health and called out jokes to each other. And the Germans called out to the French asking whether it was true that they ate frogs and the French asked the Germans whether it was true that beer makes whiskers grow. In the military headquarters the undeclared truces were tolerated because

SOLDIERS
SANG CAROLS

it was a way of allowing the soldiers to relax and it saved on leave passes. And later in the German High Command they decided that it was a pity not to make use of the undeclared truces solely in the interest of propaganda and information for the enemy and they started to print flyers and postcards that the German soldiers then sent across the minefields along with cigarettes. The flyers said that the English were only pretending to help the French, or that the Eastern Front no longer existed and the Russian army had been driven back beyond the Urals. And the postcards showed French soldiers taken prisoner by the Germans, and they all had tanned faces and clean uniforms.

And there were also people who looked forward to the twenty-first century and said that it was a new opportunity for mankind and we had to learn from past mistakes and create a new NEW MAN man who would be more in tune with the new times. And that if people learned from their mistakes there would be no more wars or diseases or floods or earthquakes or famines or totalitarian regimes, because the new man would be dynamic and tolerant and positive. The twentieth century was said to be the most lethal in human history, and those who looked forward to the twenty-first century said that in all events it could not be worse, but others said that it could always be worse or at least just as bad. Some people who read the Bible said that mankind was incorrigible and that everything in the Bible was written in anagrams and permutations, that it told, for instance, who would assassinate whom and when and where, and when war would break out and who would be president and where, and it said there would be, for instance, HALF A MILLION DEAD AT VERDUN and CYCLON B and THE AIDS EPIDEMIC and THE FALL OF COMMUNIST RUSSIA with all data and details, quite simply, everything that had happened and would happen, but that it was impossible to know in advance because we did not know what we were looking for, and if we knew what we were looking for, we would find it all there in time, but then it would not happen and there could be nothing there. They said that it might sound strange when someone did not understand it, but that the scales had fallen from their eyes. And some people said that the end of the world would be very soon, and others said that it would be a while yet. And anthropologists said that the end of the world was an important factor for the lives of individuals and communities, because it helped banish fear and aggression and reconcile one with one's own death. And psychologists said that it was important for individuals to be able to vent their aggression and the best way was through competitive sports, because everyone participating vented their aggression and there were far less deaths than in war.

In the years 1944 and 1945, half a million women fought in the German army and some of them worked in special mine-clearing units so that the German soldiers would have a retreat route and others shot down enemy aircraft bombing German cities. And four million women worked in civil defense and freed corpses from the ruins of bombed buildings and transported them to mass graves to prevent the outbreak of plague. And in some cities they held special courses about the cremation of corpses. The courses lasted four days and were organized into groups of fifteen to twenty trainees. They would learn how to operate machines for crushing bones, how to level off pits that the corpses were put into, and how to sow the land so that trees could be planted above the pits. Trees were important in cities as they ensured regeneration of oxygen and the ash from the corpses could be used as fertilizer in fruit orchards and vegetable gardens, because organic fertilizer was starting to be in short supply in Germany. The corpses in the ruins of buildings were huddled up together and sometimes two or three corpses were holding hands or hugging each other and had to be sawn apart to free them. And one woman did not want to cut apart corpses and the commander of the squad in charge of the operation wanted to have her shot for sabotage but in the meantime the soldiers who were supposed to shoot her had deserted.

Yperite was the most effective of all the poison gas and gradually replaced other gases used in warfare, such as chlorine, phosgene, chloropicrin, hydrogen cyanide or arsine, and continued to be used successfully long after the First World War. Meanwhile scientists invented other nerve gases: lewisite, tabun, sarin, soman, etc. The use of nerve gases was banned at various conferences in 1899 and 1907 and 1922 and 1925 and 1946 and 1954 and 1972 and 1990 and 1992. On the battlefronts and in the rear anti-gas training was carried out and soldiers and civilians learned how to attach gas masks as fast as possible and make sure that dirt or dust from debris did not get into the filter. And in 1915, the French invented special gas masks for horses and in 1922, the Germans invented special gas masks for dogs too. And at the end of the century doctors invented preventive medicines to treat gas poisoning, but after a while it emerged that medicines to treat gas poisoning caused hepatitis and tuberculosis and migraines and memory loss. During the Second World War, the Germans manufactured 18,000 tons of poison gas per year, but the German strategists concluded that the use of poison gas would slow down troop advances and subsequent troop withdrawals. The Germans used gas to exterminate Gypsies and Jews in the

USE OF
POISON GAS

concentration camps and invented a gas known as cyclon B, which enabled large numbers of people to be killed cheaply and quickly. Because of its composition, cyclon B was classified as a disinfectant product and was first tested in February 1940 on 250 Gypsy children in the Buchenwald concentration camp who had been arrested in Brno by Czech police, and the test proved that it was more suitable than other gases for the given purpose.

One great disappointment of the twentieth century was that compulsory schooling and technological progress and scholarship and culture did not result in better or more caring people as was strongly believed in the nineteenth century, and that lots of killers and torturers and mass murderers were art lovers and listened to opera and went to exhibitions and wrote poetry and studied the humanities and medicine, etc. And among philosophers the opinion increasingly spread that the twenti-

END OF HUMANISM

eth century had marked the end of the era of humanism and a new era had commenced, which they called post-humanist, as it was not yet clear how to define it. Historians and philosophers said that humanism had been a culture of writing, which enabled society to be governed like a literary community, and that with the advent of radio after 1918 and television after 1945 this was no longer true. And that biotechnology had dealt humanism its death blow. And some said that this was all right, that humanism had been an enormous delusion in the history of human thinking, and that for centuries it had been impossible to make superior people, and that biotechnology

MAN'S OPTIMIZATION

provided a new opportunity for man's optimization, because for the first time in the history of humanity prenatal selection was now conceivable, and that the most immediate task for the future was to find the appropriate optimization code. And others said this was untrue, that humanism had optimized man by making him responsible for his actions and that had been a great step forward. But more and more people considered that responsibility was out of date and that in reality it had already been replaced by efficiency and expediency. And the new man would not be responsible but efficient. Efficiency was part of the natural order of things, whereas responsibility was a humanist invention and an alibi for inefficiency.

NEW MAN

After the First World War, Communism and Fascism spread through Europe because lots of people believed that the old world was rotten and it was necessary to seek new paths, and that democratic rule was not capable of preventing a world war and that capitalism has provoked the economic crisis. The Communists and Fascists said that it was necessary to devise a new man who would be proud and strong and hardworking and honorable and would have a sense of higher justice and of life as part of a collective. Higher justice meant that people were not entirely equal, as maintained by democratic regimes, whose constitutions recognized the same rights for every citizen. The Communists and Fascists considered human rights as a front for the interests of the bourgeoisie, which exploited the workers. And they said it was necessary to rid the world of the bourgeois canker so as to do away with the old world for good and establish a new one. The Fascists said that in the new world everyone would be a worker in the same way that everyone was once a Christian, and the Communists said that the new world would be ruled by a classless society in which everyone would work for the good of all. And they said that Communism was the natural final phase of human history. And people would do manual work in the morning and mental work in the afternoon. The first Communist Party was

THE WORLD
WAS ROTTEN

formed in 1918 in the Soviet Union and the first Fascist party
was formed in 1919 in Italy and from Italy Fascism spread
throughout Europe because people had the feeling that political power was corrupt and that the multi-party system simply
cost money and nobody got anything out of it. Communists
and Fascists said that the multi-party system and democracy
led to the degeneration of society and the destruction of values.

DESTRUCTION
OF VALUES

And when they would be in power they would ensure everyone
a comfortable and happy life, except for those who did not
deserve it, and it was necessary to ensure the free development
of the healthy core of society and get rid of the parasites, who
clung to the old world because they were incapable of revolutionary thinking. And in Germany Nazism developed, which
promoted racial purity, and this meant that Aryans must not
mix with inferior races lest they pollute the Aryan bloodline.
Aryans were identifiable by being white and blond and the
ratio of the length of their skulls to their width was less than

SENSE OF
COMMUNITY

75 and they were endowed with a creative spirit and a sense
of community. The Nazis said that nature was cruel but just.
And they said that the person who wanted to enforce new revolutionary ideas and values and higher justice had to be cruel
and just. And that history was an eternal struggle between
truth and lies. And they were the truth. And everyone had to
choose which side to be on, because otherwise the hurricane
of history would sweep them aside.

The Nazis invented gas chambers and the use of cyclon B,
which allowed them to kill large numbers of people cheaply
and quickly in order to preserve the Aryan race from degeneration. The Nazis considered that the Aryan race was the best
of all and they were the best of all the Aryan races because
they knew how to wage war and conduct trade and organize

convivial entertainments. And they said that Europe was dec- EUROPE WAS DECADENT adent but they would prevent its disintegration since it would be a great mistake to leave Europe in decline until it finally disintegrated. And it was necessary to rid Europe of those that were good for nothing, Gypsies and Slavs and lunatics and homosexuals, etc., but chiefly Jews, because Jews wanted to JEWS WANTED TO DEFILE EUROPE defile Europe. And in Germany and the occupied territories they rounded up the Jews and took them to concentration camps and there they stripped them and sent them to special facilities known as gas chambers. They were large halls with a single entrance and without windows, and pipes ran along the ceilings, and when they had crowded people into the halls they released gas at them from the pipes and the people suffocated. And they pulled the gold teeth out of the mouths of the gassed people and some of them were skinned and their skin was used to make lampshades for top-ranking officers and important political leaders. And before they sent them to the gas chambers their heads were shaved and the hair was then used to stuff mattresses or to make dolls' wigs. And scientists discovered how to make soap for German soldiers from the fat of the gassed people. Ten liters of water was added to five kilograms of fat and a kilo of caustic soda, the mixture was boiled in a cauldron for three hours, a little salt was added, it was allowed to simmer and left to cool, when a skin formed, which was removed, cut up and allowed to simmer once more, and before it cooled down again a special solution was added so that the soap did not smell. In Gdansk, one German soldier GERMAN SOLDIER WENT MAD IN GDANS went mad because before the war he had had a mistress and did not know she was Jewish and afterwards she was taken to Auschwitz, and his friends told him as a joke that the soap they had been using for a week was from that mistress, that they had found out about it from the director of the Gdansk anatomical institute, where they took the corpses to be turned into soap. And afterwards that soldier had to be taken to a mental hospital in Germany.

Eventually most believers came to accept that the Bible was symbolic rather than scientific and that perhaps the creation of the world was not entirely clear, but it made no difference because the Bible was actually an allegory and the allegory was the key to the order of the universal and human fate and that everyone was subject to the same higher will. And in all events there had to be something behind it. Some of them founded sects and believed in various things. Some proclaimed that man can become God, and believed in a universal resurrection and created a genealogical archive to discover who would be who when the time came. Others did not eat meat and did not drink alcohol and awaited the imminent arrival of Christ and looked forward to going to Paradise, and yet others believed that there was light hidden in every person, and if they would meditate a lot, the Holy Spirit would light the light within them. And the best known were the Jehovah's Witnesses and the Pentecostalists and the Amish, who did not like electricity and used kerosene lamps for lighting and went around in dark clothes and declared that technical achievements had the effect of distancing people from God, and distancing people from God was the objective of the Antichrist, who sought to destroy the soul in people. Jehovah's Witnesses did not believe in the immortality of the spirit, but believed that after death they would return to Earth and would live in eternal bliss, and the twenty-two Biblical patriarchs would return with them, and after the war they built a big house in California for them. And people would forget terrestrial languages and would communicate by the power of faith and thoughts. And at the end of the century apocalyptic sects that wanted to hasten the

UNIVERSAL
RESURRECTION

apocalypse and build a new and better world that would only be entered by those who had seen the light in time proliferated. And the more the number of Christians declined, the greater the number of people who believed that some god existed but it GOD EXISTED was necessary to seek it elsewhere. And yet other people believed that life on Earth, or at least man, had been created through the intervention of extraterrestrial forces, that some extraterrestrials had once landed on Earth long ago and sprayed oxygen into the atmosphere or inseminated some ape or other in order to create an intelligent creature. And in 1954 an American invented Scientology. And he said that Scientology was the one true path to freedom that would enable the liberation of mankind as a whole. And he said that the world was not created by God but people. They had created it a long time ago at the time when people were immortal spiritual beings. However in the course of creating the world an accident occurred and people lost their power and degenerated to such an extent that they forgot they were immortal and spiritual. But Scientology could liberate them from the shackles of matter, space, and time and LIBERATION FROM THE help them rediscover their awareness of themselves and thereby SHACKLES OF MATTER their lost power also.

At the beginning of the century there was a strong belief in positivism and electricity and inventions and biology and mammalian evolution and psychology and social physics, known as sociology, and scientists concluded that by the use of the latest discoveries and resources made available to mankind by modern science it would be possible to breed man to perfection and so build a new, more rational and humane MORE HUMAN WORLD world. And at the turn of the twentieth century eugenics, which studied ways of perfecting the human species, became widespread. Eugenicists said that in the human race, alongside fit and healthy individuals, there also existed unfit individuals, the insane and criminals and drunkards and prostitutes, etc., and the latter impeded the development of the human species. And they recommended that governments publish legislation enabling the elimination from the development of the human species those who were biologically defective and suffered from innate and inherited tendencies to asocial behavior. And they said that biologically defective individuals should be sterilized HEALTHY CORE in order to eliminate the defect and leave the core healthy. And they drew up statistics and said that, for instance, an eighty-three-year-old alcoholic woman would have a total of 894 offspring, 67 of which would be criminal recidivists, 7 murderers, 181 prostitutes, 142 beggars and 40 lunatics, a total ASOCIAL ELEMENTS of 437 asocial elements. And they calculated that those 437 asocial elements would cost society as much as the building of 140 apartment houses. The Nazis later concluded that even sterilization and castration and forced abortions and special residential institutions cost society money that could be used more appropriately and that it was simpler to eliminate the asocial elements from the development of the human species by euthanasia. And over 200,000 asocial elements were interned in concentration camps and killed in gas chambers, which enabled the Nazis to set in operation and test the gas chambers even before the final solution to the Jewish problem was proclaimed. The asocial elements in the concentration camps wore a black triangle on their chest while the Jews wore a yellow star. And political prisoners wore a red triangle and homosexuals, who constituted a separate category of asocial elements, wore a pink triangle.

After the First World War memorials to the fallen soldiers started to be built, lest they be forgotten. Historians said that war memorials had existed before the First World War, but not until the 1920s had they become a universally shared symbol of remembrance and sculptors and masons were glad they received lots of commissions. War memorials were mostly built in the shape of steles or obelisks. At the top was a cockerel or St. George or an eagle depending on the nationality of the fallen soldiers, in the middle an armed soldier with a calm and determined expression and at the bottom women and children, and anthropologists and ethnologists said that this was typical for Indo-European culture. The names of the fallen soldiers were often listed alphabetically. The most frequent words on the memorials were HOMELAND, HEROS, MARTYRS, and REMEMBER! Sometimes the memorials also bore the inscription A CURSE ON WAR! And in some cities monuments were also built to the soldiers condemned to death or to forced labor during the war for refusing to obey orders. And at Juvincourt in 1916 a soldier was executed for not having regulation trousers and refusing to take the trousers of a dead comrade because they were dirty and blood-stained. And in 1920, the French came up with the idea of a monument to the Unknown Soldier with an eternal flame which enjoyed great success, particularly in England and Belgium and Italy and also those new countries that had no history yet, such as Czechoslovakia, Yugoslavia, etc. An unknown soldier was a soldier whose head was blown off by an explosion, or whose identity tag had been shattered by an enemy bullet, or a soldier who had been buried in a landslide, or a soldier who had got stuck in a bog. One Belgian soldier sank into a bog near Courtai right up to his knees and four of his comrades were unable to drag him out and by then all the horses were dead. And when they were retreating by the same route two days later, the soldier was still alive, but only his head was showing and he was not shouting anymore.

INDO-EUROPEAN CULTURE

THE UNKNOWN SOLDIER

THE HORSES WERE DEAD

*

And when the Nazis lost the war, the victorious countries organized an international trial and the lawyers pondered about what name to give to the final solution of the Jewish question and the various plans for the extermination of the Gypsies, Slavs, etc., and they invented the term genocide. Historians concluded that in the twentieth century about sixty genocides had occurred in the world, but not all of them entered historical memory. Historians said that historical memory was not part of history and memory was shifted from the historical to the psychological sphere, and this instituted a new mode of memory whereby it was no longer a question of memory of events but memory of memory. And the psychologization of memory aroused in people a feeling that they had to pay some kind of debt to the past, but what or to whom was not obvious. The final solution of the Jewish question was later called the Holocaust or Shoah, because the Jews said that it was not exactly genocide, but something else that went beyond genocide, something that went beyond human understanding, and they said that it was specific to the Jews, and lots of people had the feeling that the Jews were appropriating genocide and said that the victims of any genocide perceived their experience as something that went beyond human understanding, and that the Jews were confusing historical reality with its representation and so paradoxically they helped ensure that most people imagined the Holocaust like some dramatic scene from a film. And some rabbis said that the Jews had not died in the concentration camps by accident or mistake, but that it was a reincarnation of souls that sinned in other lives, because only a few souls remained God-fearing and unblemished throughout their life on Earth. And historians said that Western society had shifted from a traditional understanding of history as a continuum of memory to a concept of memory that is

NEW MODE
OF MEMORY

projected into historical discontinuity. And yet other rabbis said that during the Holocaust God had withdrawn from the scene, but it was not a punishment as such, but the return of the earth to its original state before God imposed order upon it and darkness was upon the face of the deep. And one Jewish young woman survived the war because on the railroad platform at the Struthof concentration camp she played an aria from *The Merry Widow* on the violin. And historians said that the age of identity had finally come to a close, because historiography had entered the epistemological era.

THE MERRY WIDOW

The Nazis started to consider a final solution of the Jewish question in 1940 when they decided to deport all the European Jews to Madagascar. The only Jews to remain in Europe would be those who had influential and rich relatives in America and the Argentine, and the Nazis estimated that there were about 10,000 Jews with influential and rich relatives in America and the Argentine and they were to be placed in a special concentration camp and about nine million Jews were to be deported to Madagascar, where reservations with internal self-government would be set up, and the Jews would be among their own and would gradually degenerate, because Nature had expelled them from her bosom and without the supply of Aryan blood which they obtained in Europe they would eventually die out. The idea of deporting the Jews to Madagascar first appeared in 1905 in a book by a Viennese exegete who studied the Old Testament and zoology and invented a field of study he called theozoology. And he came to the conclusion that God did not exist and that the world was created by gods, who were of the same species as people, but were capable of transmitting electric signals, and had mastered telepathy and were immortal and spiritual, but in the course of time they started to mix

JEWS TO MADAGASCAR

THEOZOOLOGY

with people and animals and became mortal. And he said that
the closest to the gods and the first generation of god people
were the Aryans, who still displayed remnants of electronic
power and telepathic neutrons, and he proposed deporting the
Jews to Madagascar and setting up ZUCHTKLÖSTER, breeding
convents, in Germany, where German women inseminated by
Aryan males would be, and so god people would be re-bred
and they would communicate telepathically by the power of
thought and electrical charges. In the end, the Nazis concluded
that deportation to Madagascar would cost money that was
needed to support the war effort, and in 1942 they decided
that the final solution would henceforth consist in extermi-
nating the Jews by all available means.

People traveled in sealed freight cars that remained closed
throughout the journey and they had nowhere to go to the
toilet, and when someone died, the corpse remained in the
car. Some concentration camps were intended for labor and
others for extermination of the Jews, who were a threat to the
Aryan race. When people arrived at the extermination camps,
the Germans divided them into two or three groups, men and
women separately, and sometimes children separately too, and
they ordered them to strip naked and took away their clothes.
Sometimes the Germans selected someone when they needed
new laborers or a translator or a pretty young servant girl, and
they sent the rest to the gas chambers. From their descent
from the train to the gas chambers it took the men ten min-
utes and the women a quarter of an hour, because the women
had longer and thicker hair and it took longer to shave them.
The shaved-off hair was then used as stuffing for mattresses
and for manufacturing dolls' wigs, and lest the people on the
railroad platform start to riot the Germans told them that

first of all they would be going into the baths, and sometimes they handed out tickets and told the people they would have to present them at the ticket office of the baths. And on the surrounding buildings there were signs with the words BUFFET, TICKET OFFICE, TELEGRAPH, etc., and the people, although they were scared, thought they were at a railroad station and would be taken elsewhere and that the stripping and head shaving were necessary for hygienic reasons, because the Germans were very hygienically-minded, and for one hundred kilograms of hair the camp administration received five Reichsmarks from the State. And they said to themselves that as soon as they had washed they would go to another camp, where they would work, because hard work was the best path to reform. People entered the gas chambers with their hands above their heads so that there would be room for more of them, and at the last minute they bundled in the children, who were smaller and did not take up so much room. Sometimes a band made up of young women prisoners in white blouses and blue sailors' skirts would stand on the railroad platform singing operatic arias.

GERMANS WERE HYGIENICALL MINDED

The first genocide of the twentieth century took place in Turkey in 1915. The government first arrested and shot 600 Armenian families living in Constantinople and disarmed and shot soldiers of Armenian origin serving in the Turkish army. And all the Armenians received orders to evacuate the city and villages within twenty-four or forty-eight hours and the Turkish army took up position at the city gates and as the people were coming out all the men were shot and all the women and children were sent into exile in desert areas of Mesopotamia. And the women and children had to march three to five hundred kilometers on foot without food, and most of them died. And the French and the English and the Russians sent a protest note, which, for the first time in history, spoke about a crime

RIME AGAINST HUMANITY

against humanity. And one German officer, who was serving in the Turkish army at the time as an instructor, brought sixty-six photographs of the Armenian massacre to Germany and sent them to the German Kaiser, and wrote to him that Germany should pick its allies more carefully because Turkey's shame rubbed off on it too. And in the years 1928 to 1949, the Russians deported six million people of suspect nationality—Armenians and Tartars and Lithuanians and Estonians and Ukrainians and Poles and Germans and Moldavians and Greeks and Koreans and Kalmyks and Kurds and Ingush, etc. And 30% of them died on the journey and 20% died during the following year. The Communists later said that they were not deportations but optimization of geographical space and the first step toward a new supranational society, in which it would not be important who lived where, but how hard they worked for the common good. And in 1934, they devised a reservation for the Jews and they invited all Soviet Jews to move there. The reservation lay on the border with China in the region of Khabarovka, and in winter the temperature there fell to -40°, and the Communists said it was not a reservation but an autonomous region, where the Jews could be among their own and have their own self-government. And in 1944, they deported to Kazakhstan and Kyrgyzstan 477,000 Chechens in 12,525 cattle trucks and 190,000 Chechens died on the journey from hunger and frost and in 1999 they devised special camps for suspect Chechens that were called interim

RESETTLEMENT CAMPS

resettlement camps. And in 1948, journalists and doctors and engineers of Jewish origin were accused of cosmopolitanism and Zionism and bourgeois thinking and they had most of them murdered and others were sent to concentration camps.

The number of victims of the Armenian genocide was estimated at one to one-and-a-half million, but the Turks said that the Armenian genocide was not a real genocide and most Jews agreed.

Scientologists said that man was essentially good, but some people were better than others, and they divided mankind into four groups. The best were the Scientologists, because they knew things that others did not know. In the second group was the majority of mankind that had not yet seen the light, and a fifth of mankind consisted of people known as POTENTIAL TROUBLE SOURCES, and those were people who said that Scientologists were crazy and two-and-a-half percent of mankind consisted of SUPPRESSIVE PERSONS, and these were people who wanted to suppress truth and prevent mankind from liberating itself. And the Scientologists thought of seventy-two ways of exposing them so that, at the moment when the spiritual transformation of the old world occurred, they did not mingle with the others. The Scientologists devised special security detachments whose members were recruited for a period of a billion years to expose those who did not want the liberation of mankind. The Scientologists said that mankind would sooner or later be liberated, but it could still take some time. And they said that people could achieve self-enlightenment during their life on earth and so achieve their return to spirituality and immortality, but first of all it was necessary for one to free oneself from the shackles of matter and time. People freed of their shackles could travel back in time as many as 75 million years and comprehend all the traumas they had gone through during that period. It was the fault of the traumas that they had lost their energy. And if they wanted to find the energy they lost on account of the traumas, they first

TRANS-
FORMATION
OF THE OLD
WORLD

RETURN TO
SPIRITUALIT

of all had to erase from their consciousness the engrams that preserved traces of human memory. Once they had erased the engrams they could rid themselves of their memory and their human fate and travel in time and achieve self-enlightenment.

The first law on the sterilization of defective and asocial elements was enacted in 1907 in the United States. The law permitted the sterilization of hardened criminals and the mentally ill and in 1914, at the urging of psychiatrists, it was extended to recidivist robbers and alcoholics and in 1923, in Missouri, it was extended to chicken thieves of Negro and Indian origin, because in the case of chicken thieves of white origin, the opinion was that they could still find a way back and reintegrate themselves into the life of society through hard and conscientious work. And in 1929, a sterilization law was enacted in Switzerland and Denmark and in 1934 in Norway and in 1935 in Finland and Sweden, and in Sweden it remained in force until 1975, and 13,810 Swedish men and 48,955 Swedish women were sterilized by court order. In countries with a Catholic tradition, eugenic laws did not exist, because Catholics were opposed to the theory of evolution and sterilization and abortions and they said that no one has the right to take away from people what they had received from God, and Protestants, on the other hand, said that mentalities evolve and that it was typical that the Catholics rejected progress and they had been saying so for four hundred years already. In the Communist countries, the sterilization of defective individuals simply required a doctor's recommendation and in Yugoslavia and Romania and Czechoslovakia, Albanian and Gypsy women were surreptitiously sterilized too because the governments of those countries concluded that the numbers of Albanians and Gypsies in the socialist camp were growing out of proportion. In Germany a sterilization law was enacted in 1933, when the Nazis came to power and the first to be sterilized were children known as RHEINLANDSBASTARDE, Rhineland bastards, who were children whose mothers were German and BASTARDS their fathers Negroes from the French army which was then in occupation of the Rhineland. And 514 Rhineland bastards were sterilized and sent to mental hospitals and the mothers of the Rhineland bastards were convicted of collaboration with the enemy and subversion of the German state and sent to the SUBVERSION OF THE STATE Ravensbrück concentration camp. The camp at Ravensbrück was a special concentration camp for women and later women were also sent for committing subversion of the state with prisoners of war or laborers from occupied countries working in German factories or on German farms, and 92,350 women died in Ravensbrück. And at the Dachau concentration camp doctors were provided with a low-pressure chamber in which they investigated the behavior of epileptic children and tried to establish the difference between hereditary and non-hereditary epilepsy. And in 1910, the Americans devised a Eugenics Board, and in 1922, the Director of the American board sent the U.S. government a list of socially inadaptable citizens who INADAPTABLE CITIZENS should be sterilized in order to preserve a healthy and fit society. The list was divided into ten groups according to various medical and social criteria and included citizens dependent on society and citizens without fixed abode or sufficient income and citizens suffering from a congenital defect or chronic and infectious diseases and citizens with very poor vision or a severe hearing defect and tramps and madmen and psychopaths and criminals and prostitutes and homosexuals and syphilitics and alcoholics and drug addicts and consumptives and epileptics. Doctors also investigated whether there was any difference between epilepsy in people and epilepsy in rabbits, which the camp administration ordered from Vienna. And in Vienna, on the other hand, they ordered corpses from the Mauthausen concentration camp for the Anatomical Institute and the medical faculties. The corpses had to be fresh and undamaged and the Anatomical Institute used to order on average 460 undamaged corpses per year, most of which were used for dissection in anatomy courses. And in Norway after the war they took away from unmarried mothers children whose fathers were German soldiers and sent them to mental hospitals. And lots of biologists and geneticists and psychiatrists and anthropologists believed that, alongside electricity, eugenics was modern science's greatest contribution to mankind and just as electricity had transformed people's material conditions and enabled the world to enter a new epoch, eugenics for its part would radically transform society's biological base and enable the world to enter a new era. But some eugenicists said that sterilization served no purpose and calculated that it would take twenty-two generations to reduce the number of lunatics and psychopaths by 0.9%, and a further ninety generations before the proportion of lunatics and psychopaths in society stabilized at one in a hundred thousand. And they said it was necessary to find a quicker means of making mankind healthier.

With the emancipation of women and the invention of contraception and tampons and disposable diapers there were fewer children in Europe but more toys and kindergartens and slides and climbing frames and dogs and hamsters, etc. Sociologists said that the child had become the center of attention in the family and gradually its most influential component also. And children wanted to be independent and have their own identity and did not want to wear their older siblings' hand-me-down caps or shoes and they always wanted new caps and

ANATOMY
COURSES

STERILIZATION
SERVED NO
PURPOSE

CHILDREN
WANTED TO BE
INDEPENDENT

shoes and colored pencils and construction sets and teddy bears and dolls. In the European countries twelve-and-a-half thousand times more dolls were manufactured in the twentieth century than in the nineteenth century and instead of wood and sawdust they were made of plastics and in the course of time they learnt to whimper and talk and were more and more independent, and they would say GOOD MORNING and ENJOY YOUR MEAL, for instance, and some of them could weep and burp after eating or sing part of an aria. The best-known doll was called Barbie and was first manufactured in 1959. It was 30 centimeters tall and had big breasts and hips and a slim waist and was the first doll to behave like an adult. Soon it started to talk too and said I'VE GOT A DATE WITH MY BOYFRIEND THIS EVENING and WHAT WILL I WEAR TO THE DANCE? and WOULD YOU LIKE TO GO CLOTHES SHOPPING WITH ME? At first she was dressed like a ballerina or an actress or a model, then later as a stewardess, a teacher, a veterinarian, a businesswoman, an astronaut, or a presidential candidate. And in 1986, a Barbie doll appeared dressed in a striped concentration-camp uniform and a striped cap too. Various ex-prisoners associations protested and said it made a mockery of the suffering and the memory of the victims, and the manufacturers answered back and said that, on the contrary, it was an appropriate way of acquainting the younger generation with the suffering in the concentration camps, and that little girls who bought the doll in the striped uniform would identify with it and later, when they were grown up, they would more easily comprehend what sort of suffering there was. And in 1998 the Germans came up with the idea of erecting in Berlin a large monument to the victims of the Holocaust, which was to be visible from afar, because, in addition to celebrating some positive historical event, the function of a monument is also

ASSOCIATIONS PROTESTED

to be a warning to future generations. Some people thought
that an art object was not the proper way of expressing the
Holocaust, which defies all aesthetic rules, and others concluded that the ideal project would be one that expressed the
fact that the Holocaust defied expression. And four hundred
and ninety-five artists sent various proposals for expressing a
warning to future generations and one proposed manufacturing a large, eight-colored, six-pointed star turning on its own
axis, and others proposed constructing an enormous Ferris
wheel, on which concentration-camp wagons would be hung
in place of the usual fair-ground cars, and others proposed
constructing a large bus station with red buses and timetables
on which the terminal stations would be the names of concentration camps, and others proposed erecting thirty-nine steel
posts on which why? would be written in various languages,
WARUM?, WAAROM?, VARFØR?, PROČ?, POURQUOI?, PERCHÉ?,
DLACZEGO?, CŪR?, KUIDA?, MIKSI?, MIÉRT?, ZAKAJ?, KODĖL?,
HVORFOR?, JIATÍ?, PSE?, NIÇIN?, etc. Some people were of the
opinion that it ought to be a monument to the victims not
only of the Holocaust, but of all possible genocides, because
only in that way would it contain the living historical memory,
otherwise it would be simply a heap of steel or iron that would
say nothing to anyone within twenty or so years. And some
historians said that building monuments was problematic in
all events, because preserving the memory of some event did
not of itself guarantee that it would not be repeated, and they
provided instances of preserving memory that had led to fresh
conflicts and wars.

The Jews who survived the Holocaust said that monuments
and museums, etc., were important, but that best of all were
direct testimonies, and they would visit schools to tell the
pupils what they had gone through. And they wondered how

WARNING
TO FUTURE
GENERATIONS

ERRIS WHEEL

PRESERVING
MEMORY

to preserve the memory of the Holocaust after their deaths, and the Swedish association of former Jewish prisoners recommended passing on their testimony to some young person, who would learn it by heart and visit schools and tell the pupils that they had known someone who had experienced such and such. And before they died they would pass the testimony on to another young person, etc. And in 1945, the Jews issued an appeal to public opinion, requesting the establishment of an Israeli state in Palestine, where the Jews could be among their own and would not have to fear any more holocausts. And they fought against the Arabs and the English, who were occupying Palestine at the time, and organized assassinations and illicit immigration operations. And in 1939, the English decreed immigration quotas that reduced the number of Jewish immigrants by 75% and enacted a law prohibiting Jews from buying land. And in 1947, a ship docked in Palestine with illegal Jewish immigrants from Germany and the English sent it back again. And in 1938, the Swedish government requested the German authorities to insert a capital J in passports for Jews, so that the Swedish frontier police could recognize a Jew who did not look like one. The ship that docked in Palestine was called EXODUS after a book of the Old Testament and 4,500 Jews were sailing in her, having survived the concentration camps and wanting to return to the Promised Land. And in November, the United Nations voted in favor of the creation of the State of Israel. And lots of people in Europe traveled to Israel to see the new state in creation. And young people from Europe went to work in Jewish agricultural communes known as KIBBUTZIM, where everyone worked for the good of all. And everything was shared and everyone sang songs together. And the Israeli travel agencies issued posters on which young people with serious expressions observed the sun rising over Jerusalem, and underneath was written OUR SUFFERING WAS

JEWS IN PALESTINE

EVERYTHING WAS SHARED

NOT IN VAIN and TAKE ADVANTAGE OF LOW PRICES.

Sexologists said that the Barbie doll was the first tool for inculcating a feminine identity in young girls, and the doll's successful reception proved that child sexuality existed. Child sexuality was much spoken about in the twentieth century after it was discovered that little girls would like to have a child with their father, which was actually a substitute penis because little girls would like a penis too, and the doll was a child from their father and a penis at the same time. For a long time only little girl dolls were made but then they started to manufacture little boy dolls, and little girl dolls had a groove between their legs and little boy dolls had a little penis. And in the seventies, they started to manufacture black or brown dolls, although they were mostly bought by white parents who wanted to show their children they were not racists. Racism was a theory from the nineteenth century that said that the human races have immutable characteristics, and they were at different levels of development and the most developed were the white race which had an innate sense of social organization and abstract thought and convivial entertainment, and a racist was someone who feared that mixing between races jeopardized the specific characteristics of the white race and eroded the genetic potential that enabled the whites to continue advancing in the forefront of mankind. People who did not like Jews were not racists but anti-Semites, because the Jews were not strictly regarded as inferior, like Negroes, Indians, Gypsies, etc., but more of a natural aberration. The word anti-Semite appeared at the end of the nineteenth century and denoted a person who did not want the Jews to rule the world and called on their fellow citizens to resist. Racism became a major social problem after the Second World War because large ethnic minorities settled in the rich European countries, and society had to absorb them. There

DOLLS WITH
LITTLE PENIS

CALLS TO
RESIST

existed two models for absorbing ethnic minorities—integration and assimilation, and integration was adopted by countries that believed that various cultural models could coexist within civil society and that it was better not to mix one with another and for each of them to preserve its specific character, and assimilation was implemented by countries that believed in universalism and were of the opinion that there existed a higher social interest that took precedence over specific ethnic and cultural characteristics. For a long while it looked as if the assimilation model was more successful, because in the countries that implemented it there were no race riots such as there were in England, America, etc., but at the end of the century, when people started to talk about globalism, universalism went out of fashion and everybody wanted to have their own identity and be proud of their race, but not in the sense of race, but civilization and live in accordance with traditions and return to their roots, etc.

UNIVERSALISM WENT OUT OF FASHION

Sex became very important in Europe in the twentieth century, more important than religion and almost as important as money, and everyone wanted to have sexual intercourse in different ways and some men rubbed their sexual organ with cocaine to prolong their erection even though cocaine was banned in all circumstances. And after the Second World War films started to include scenes in which the leading characters had sexual intercourse, which was previously considered improper because lots of people still believed in God and sexual intercourse was generally only hinted at by a shot of a bed or a clock or the sky, or it suddenly went dark. And women wanted to have orgasms all the time and that made men nervous and they had problems with erections and tried various aphrodisiacs and attended psychoanalysis to discover where the problem lay, such as whether they might have suffered some childhood

PROBLEMS WITH ERECTIONS

trauma that they were unaware of. Psychoanalysis was invented
in 1900 by a Viennese neurologist who wanted to study mental
processes and evaluate subjects by means of the unconscious,
and he came to the conclusion that neurosis, hysteria, etc.,
were symptoms of sexual traumas in childhood, and he devised
REPETITIVE
COMPULSION for this purpose new methods and concepts such as repetitive
compulsion, regression, repression, ego, superego, libido and
complexes, which could be either Oedipal or castration complexes. And in 1938 he fled from the Nazis to London and four
of his sisters died in concentration camps. And when patients
knew why they were depressed and neurotic they immediately
felt better because it was normal. Communists said that people
who lived in a Communist society had no need for sex because
people's greatest happiness should be from work well done,
whereas in capitalism people did not get enjoyment from their
work because they were exploited and therefore resorted to various surrogates. And they said that without class consciousness
sex could not bring satisfaction even it were repeated endlessly
and they were afraid that if people were to attend psychoanaly-
COHESION OF
THE SOCIALIST
CAMP sis and resort to surrogates it would threaten the cohesion of the
socialist camp. And they did not want people to read decadent
books or wear garish clothes, have eccentric hairstyles, chew
gum, etc. Chewing-gum was invented by an American phar-
macist and was first sold in Europe in 1903, although its use
spread mainly in the fifties and sixties. It was mostly chewed
by young people, who thereby expressed their attitude towards
society and didn't have fillings in their mouths yet.

In the fifties film heroes usually had sexual intercourse in cornfields because cornfields were associated with youth and the
WIND RUFFLED
THE CORN new life awaiting the young heroes, and wind ruffled the ears
of corn as the sun sank on the horizon and women's bosoms

heaved, and in the sixties film heroes had sexual intercourse in the surf on the ocean shore because it was romantic and sand clung to their skin, and their bottoms could be seen, and mist hung over the water. In the sixties, the first pornographic films were also made, in which people had sexual intercourse almost non-stop in various places. And in magazines for girls, woman editors with greater experience explained how to perform fellatio, etc. And in magazines for boys, editors with greater experience explained how to avoid premature ejaculation and put on a condom discreetly. And advertising agencies created advertisements for condoms and thought of ways of attracting young viewers and one agency devised commercials in which various fairy-tale characters, such as Snow White, Cinderella, Donkey Skin, Scheherazade, etc., had sexual intercourse. And in art films there was more and more sexual intercourse, but the critics said that it was something else, because it was not sexual intercourse as such but its representation. And when there was lots of sexual intercourse in some art film, they said that the film expressed our entomological attitude toward love, which was fine because it enabled us to reflect more effectively on the role of sexual intercourse not only in an anthropological, cultural or political context, but also in human life. In the seventies film heroes mostly had sexual intercourse in motor cars, because it was original and the speed of life was increasing all the time, and young people who did not have cars could imagine what was in store for them one day. And men increasingly lay on their backs and women sat on them because they were now emancipated. And in the eighties, telephone sex started and men called certain numbers to hear women say into the mouthpiece I'M GETTING WET or STUFF IT RIGHT IN ME or WILL YOU LET ME TASTE IT?, etc.

HOW TO
ATTRACT
YOUNG VIEWE

LIFE
ACCELERATES

*

Psychoanalysis became widespread in Western Europe in the sixties and seventies and people entered therapy who were not ill but felt helpless and abandoned and wanted to know if they had any traumas. And when patients had got over their shyness and relaxed, they would tell the psychoanalyst about their childhood, and that was called displacement, because eventually they would recollect something they had purged from their memory during childhood, because they did not realize that in mental life everything survived, and that although something might be purged from memory for a while, it survived somewhere, and so the patient would give the psychoanalyst verbal clues that the psychoanalyst could follow. Displacement was when some little boy or girl had an urge that was at odds with morality and so they banished the instinct to their subconscious, but when they grew up and became adults, they could have strange dreams, for instance, which showed they had a trauma. And the Oedipus complex was when a little girl wanted to kill her mother in order to have sexual intercourse with her father, or a little boy wanted to kill his father in order to have sexual intercourse with his mother, but they knew very well it was not allowed. There were disputes among the specialists about the Oedipus complex, because some thought it was universal, while others thought it occurred only in certain cultures—in Vienna, etc. And in 1918 a congress was held in Budapest on psychoanalysis and its role in wartime, and most psychiatrists agreed that wartime neurosis had the same causes as peacetime neurosis. And various psychiatrists suggested treating neurosis with electric shock and they kept treating soldiers with electric shock until the soldiers declared they felt completely fit. But other psychiatrists did not agree with this and said that electric shock simply pushed traumas deeper into the unconscious but they did not actually cure

ISPLACEMENT

DISPUTES
AMONG
SPECIALISTS

them. And others said that soldiers faked traumas in order to SOLDIERS FAKED TRAUMAS spend the war in lunatic asylums and play cards with the other lunatics for money or cigarettes.

During the First World War there was a major expansion of humanitarian organizations and charitable associations, because the First World War was in many respects innovative and the parties involved had greater fire power and means of destruction available to them, and compulsory military service allowed large numbers of troops to be sent into war, and long-range artillery and airships and airplanes permitted military action against civilians and effective operations behind enemy lines in order to undermine enemy morale. And in 1905, twelve states signed a declaration in which they promised to protect wounded soldiers regardless of what side they were fighting on, because a soldier is not simply a member of some national entity, but also an individual entity. Some generals did not agree with this and warned against an individualistic interpretation of entity and said that soldiers were sons of the homeland and had to obey the orders of the homeland. And pacifists and humanists, on the other hand, said that the individual had to be loyal to mankind and not homeland, but some humanists considered that if the homeland was threatened it became a representative of mankind. And in 1929, various countries signed a declaration in which they promised to treat prisoners of war decently and that they would be allowed to receive letters and parcels from their families and wives and charitable associations and humanitarian organizations. And CHARITABLE ASSOCIATIONS in 1941, the Soviet government issued a declaration that it did not want any humanitarian organizations to help Soviet prisoners of war or assist them to receive letters and parcels, and the Soviet generals said that they were actually deserters, who simply usurped the title of Soviet soldier, because a Soviet soldier would sooner die than let himself be taken prisoner. Humanitarian organizations provided first aid and supplied medicines and bandages to armies, and they would make inspection trips to prisoner-of-war camps to make sure that the prisoners were treated decently, and the best known one RED CROSS was the Red Cross. And in 1942, representatives of the Swiss Red Cross learnt about the gas chambers and the concentration camps, but decided not to publish the news, because they feared that the Nazis could misuse it to discredit the humanitarian organizations and prevent their access to prisoner-of-war camps and hospitals. And in 1944, the Germans made a documentary film about life in the Terezín concentration camp for the benefit of representatives of the Red Cross and various international commissions. Two hundred seventy actors and 1,600 children acted in the film, as well as several thousand adult extras, those of whom who had light-colored hair having been excluded beforehand because they did not look Jewish SO SCHÖN enough. The film was entitled HOW NICE IT WAS IN TEREZÍN WAR ES IN TEREZÍN and in it Jews went to cafes and grew vegetables in vegetable gardens and dived into swimming pools and went to the bank to draw money and to the post office for parcels and listened to opera and discussed the meaning of European civilization at the local library. And when the filming was over, the Nazis organized eleven special convoys, and everyone who had taken part in the film was sent to the Auschwitz extermination camp. And when the Soviet prisoners of war returned home after the war, the government sent them to concentration camps to atone for their lack of fighting spirit during the war by means of hard work. And whereas in previous wars five times more soldiers died of various diseases and epidemics than in combat, during the First World War, thanks to humanitarian aid and

advances in surgery and new weapons, etc., the ratio of the
dead was reversed, and that was innovative too.   THAT WAS
                                                                   INNOVATIVE TO

The Communists and Nazis said that it was necessary to
establish a world that would correspond to the natural order
of things. Historians and anthropologists later said that
Communism and Nazism replaced religious belief with a belief
in revolution and that people supported Communism and
Nazism for the same motives, the strongest of which was the
feeling that they belonged to the elect, in whose hands the fate   THE FATE
of mankind would rest henceforth. The Nazis believed that   OF MANKIND
the harmonious world of the future would be composed of
powerful, selfless individuals linked by solidarity, and the common interest and kinship of them all would create a bulwark
against the sort of decline to which the Humanists and the
Enlightenment had brought the old world. The Communists,
on the other hand, thought that in the new world all citizens
would be mutually interchangeable and people would create
a monolithic and unbroken whole, and no one would have
private interests because everything would be shared, and that
would prevent the decline to which the selfish interests of the
ruling classes had brought the old world. And they both proclaimed the need for terror as the only successful way to fight
democracy that eroded everything and led people to become
homosexuals and Anarchists and parasites and skeptics and
individualists and alcoholics, etc. And they agitated against
homosexuals and parasites and drunkards, and in Communist   HOMOSEXUALS
Russia the children of drunkards were made to parade around ETC.
the square each Sunday with a sign around their neck saying
DADDY, STOP DRINKING. I WANT MY PLACE IN THE NEW WORLD,
and in Nazi Germany drunkards had to parade around the
square with a sign saying I'VE DRUNK MY PAY AND THERE'S

NOTHING LEFT FOR MY FAMILY. And when the drunkards did not mend their ways they were sent to concentration camps where they worked for the good of all. In the German con-centration camps the sign over the entrance read WORK SHALL MAKE YOU FREE and in the Soviet concentration camps the sign over the entrance said WORK SINGLE-MINDEDLY TO FULFILL THE PLAN. And instead of GOOD MORNING, the Communists said HONOR WORK because they thought work was important and if everyone worked Communism would be victorious world-wide. And people who instead of HONOR WORK said GOOD MORNING or HELLO or GOD BLESS YOU were suspect and their neighbors would say they were not good patriots.

And when the Nazis won the elections in 1933, they enacted laws that banned Jews from various things. Jews were not allowed to hold public office, work in the army, justice, or the media and were not allowed to go to the swimming pool or the cinema and in parks they were only allowed to sit on benches assigned to them, which were painted yellow in order to be immediately identifiable. And Jewish children were not allowed to attend school or go on merry-go-rounds, and the Nazis hoped that the Jews would realize they were not welcome in Germany and would leave for somewhere else. And the Nazis also organized exhibitions of degenerate art, ENTARTETE KUNST, at which degenerate and perverted works by Jewish or Hebraicized painters and sculptors were exhibited in order to warn the German people of the dangers inherent in art conceived by sick people. The Nazis considered art important and degenerate art was the first step toward a society in which everything would be degenerate, and that is what they wanted to warn the German people against. And they organized parades and Spartakiads with allegorical floats and pictures of human bodies and said that the German people could not live without art, because art was embedded in the German people like an axe blade in its handle, and they invited German laborers to the German opera and organized processions, etc., and said that it was not necessary to hide German art GERMAN ART away in museums and galleries and bourgeois salons, because art belonged to all. And in 1935, they passed a law forbidding mixed marriages between Jews and non-Jews to protect Aryan blood and German art from the pernicious influences of Judaism. And Jews had to wear a yellow six-pointed star in their lapels and on their backs and they were not allowed to get on buses and street cars and use Aryan laundries. And on a November night in 1938 members of the German secret police plundered Jewish shops and set fire to synagogues and harassed or killed every Jew they met in the street, in order to put fear into the Jews and hasten their departure from Germany. And the Minister of Propaganda said that it was the German people's retaliation for the assassination of the German military attaché in Paris by a Polish Jew. That night was later called Kristallnacht, or Crystal Night, because 7,200 Jewish shop windows were broken and the streets were covered in splinters of glass. And the German government ordered the Jews to pay a collective fine of one billion Reichsmarks for having aroused the just anger of the German people. And the Swiss JUST ANGER government requested the Germans to stamp the passports of Jews with a large capital J so that the frontier police could recognize a Jew who did not look like one. And in Poland, Czechoslovakia, etc., countries with large German minorities, mass deportations of Germans were organized after the war, and in Brno Germans had to wear white arm bands with a large capital G and they were not allowed to travel by street car or trolley. The Swiss government was afraid that all the

German Jews would settle in Switzerland and disrupt the ethnic cohabitation and national consensus. And Jews who had been registered as Germans before the war or who had German names were also regarded as Germans, as well as Jews who had Czech names but could not speak Czech, and the letter J denoted JUDE, Jew, and ethnic cohabitation and national consensus were the pillars of the Swiss Confederation.

OUNG PEOPLE After the Second World War young people also started to be important in democratic countries because it was the beginning of the consumer society, and when young people saw an advertisement for something youthful, they wanted their parents to buy it for them. In the consumer society, new generations of children grew up in affluence and had caps and shoes and colored pencils and construction sets and they would laugh at their parents when they told them how they used to go to school barefoot or share a cap with their siblings. And when they grew up they started to say that the consumer society enslaves people and that it was necessary to devise a new world in which no one would be enslaved. And in the sixties young people started to rebel against the consumer society and enslavement and wars and racism, etc. Young people first started to rebel in the United States because at that time the

AMERICANS WERE MORE ADVANCED Americans were waging a war in Vietnam and they were more advanced in their consumer society and had baths and a telephones and did not like Negroes very much, whereas young people said Negroes enriched mankind. The Vietnam War was the first television war in history just as the Second World War had been the first radio war in history, and Negroes were not allowed to serve in higher ranks in the army and enter toilets reserved for white citizens. In some cases toilets were reserved solely for white citizens and Blacks had to find some other toilet, and in other cases the toilets were divided into two rooms, and above one there was a sign WHITES and above the other the sign said COLORED, because a sign saying NEGROES might cause offence to Negroes. Public schools were also of two kinds, separate for whites and separate for Negroes, as well as merry-go-rounds and climbing frames and sandboxes and park benches and in some cities, telephone booths too. Advocates of the assimilation immigration model said that it was an expression of segregation and that was an inevitable result of the policy of integration, and advocates of the integration model said that it was not segregation but differentialism, and that anyway Negroes felt best among their own and did not care for the company of white citizens.

NEGROES FELT BEST

When people stopped believing in God, they started to seek ways of expressing that the world is absurd, and they invented Futurism and Expressionism and Dadaism and Surrealism and Existentialism and the Theater of the Absurd. And the Dadaists wanted to do away with art and they made art out of things that were not used before, such as wires and matches and slogans and newspaper titles and the telephone directory, etc., and they said it was new and absolute art. The Futurists wrote verse with lots of interjections such as a KARAZUK ZUK ZUK DUM DUM DUM, and they promoted expressive typography, and the Expressionists and the Dadaists wrote verse in new, unknown languages to show that all languages are equal, both comprehensible and incomprehensible ones, such as BAMBLA O FALLI BAMBLA, and the Surrealists, on the other hand, promoted automatic writing and unusual metaphors, and they wrote for instance MY CORK BATH IS LIKE YOUR WORM EYE, and they explained that the meaning of this verse spurted out of it automatically and that it was physical and metaphysical at one

KARAZUK ZUK ZUK

and the same time. The Existentialists said that metaphysics was decadent and everything was subjective, but that objectivity existed nevertheless and that we were going about it the wrong way, because the most important thing was intersubjectivity. And the main thing was for everything to be authentic and that history and the course of history were the result of the philosophical question whether people could communicate authentically and, if they could, then history could be more meaningful than previously, so long as transcendental authorities were restored. And linguists said that communication was only a question of the manner of deconstruction and that there were several ways to deconstruct. And old people said that communication was in a sorry state because people were not capable of looking each other in the eye anymore and they averted their gaze immediately they caught someone's eye and that nowadays people only looked blind people in the eye.

RESTORATION OF TRANSCENDENTAL AUTHORITIES

During the First World War nine and a half million men died and six hundred thousand women. And six million men and two hundred thousand women were crippled for life. And seven million women lost their husbands in the war and nine million children lost their fathers. And countries were indebted and governments printed money that people could buy nothing with and inflation rose and in 1923 inflation in Germany rose by 2.3 million percent and a single egg cost 810 billion marks on average and when someone went out to buy a loaf of bread they would take a wheelbarrow full of money. And lots of people wanted to change the old world at its very foundations and joined Communist and Fascist parties. And others recalled pre-war Europe and they missed the days that began to be called LA BELLE ÉPOQUE or THE GOLDEN AGE. The Golden Age were the days when the advanced industrial countries had

THE GOLDEN AGE

plenty of everything and the colonial stores sold exotic fruit and chocolate and Turkish delights and people believed that the new century would put an end to poverty and toil, and people would live in comfort and hygienically, and compulsory school attendance would make people better and more humane. In the Golden Age people were more courteous to each other and criminals were more considerate and did not fire at policemen, and young people treated each other with respect and restraint and did not have sexual intercourse until they were married, and when some young man raped a girl in the fields on her way home from work and she then became pregnant, she would put the child in an orphanage where it was cared for at the state's expense, and when some motorist ran over a chicken, he would get out of his car and pay for the chicken. And men raised their hats and did not gaze at women they did not intend to greet, and in England men would wait until a woman gave a sign that she wished to be greeted, and in France men kissed women's gloves and women dropped handkerchiefs, which men picked up and returned to the women with a bow, and women did not smoke because it would be considered raffish, and men smoked cheroots and cigars and took snuff and stroked their whiskers. And on Sunday people went to church and towns-folk used to go by train to holiday resorts and ladies wore lace bonnets and men wore checkered knickerbockers and tossed balls about in the water and laughed and the Surrealists and psychoanalysts later said that the ball was actually a sexual symbol. After the war there was an increase in the numbers of illegitimate children and orphanages and lunatic asylums, but there was a decline in snuff-taking because it was unhygienic. WHY SNUFF-TAKING DECLINED

Jehovah's Witnesses believed that Jesus had already returned to Earth at the end of the nineteenth century, but he was invisible and could be seen only by the chosen and initiated. At the beginning of the century they calculated that the pagan era would come to an end in 1914 and it would be the start MILLENNIUM of a millennium in which believers would be able to achieve salvation, and then Jesus would reveal himself to all. And when the First World War broke out in 1914 they said that it was an omen and an enormous battle had occurred in heaven and Satan had been cast down to Earth and that would be the cause of the unhappiness of the twentieth century, that this was the final test sent to us by God and the last opportunity for those who wanted to be saved. The First World War broke out when an Austrian archduke was assassinated in Sarajevo by conspir- CONSPIRATORS ators from THE BLACK HAND secret society. The conspirators had read in the press which route the archduke would take to the town hall, where the mayor would give a speech and open sandwiches prepared for him, and they lined both sides of the embankment with hand grenades and revolvers in their pock- ets and they waited for the archduke to drive by. And Austria declared war on the Serbians and the Germans declared war on the Russians and the French and the Belgians, etc. The end of the world was originally declared for 1925, but when it did not happen, the Jehovah's Witnesses said it was not particularly important, more important was who would get to heaven. And they calculated that there would be 144,000 chosen ones and they would reside in heaven and direct events on Earth. And those who would accept their teachings during their life- time would live on Earth in eternal bliss when the new world END OF THE OLD WORLD began. The new world was supposed to start after the end of the old world, which they said was near, but they no longer gave a precise date. And the Austrian police, who were said to be the best in the world, arrested the five leading conspirators and handed them over to the courts, which sentenced them to life imprisonment. The conspirators served their sentences in the prison at Teresienstadt in Bohemia, and three of them died during the war and the remaining two became national heroes after the war and one of them became a doctor of philosophy at Belgrade University and in 1937 he proposed to the Yugoslav government that they deport the Kosovo Albanians ALBANIAN ETHNIC GROU because it was an ethnic group that was not suited to the Yugoslav Federation, and when he died in 1990, the Serbians closed the Albanian schools in Kosovo and banned Albanian newspapers and disbanded Albanian political associations and created a people's militia whose task was to make the Albanians realize they were unwelcome in Yugoslavia. The best means of making the Albanians realize this were terrorist operations, the burning of houses, looting of shops, etc., and the Western governments decided that this was actually genocide and launched air raids on Serbia to force the Serbian government to negotiate. The air raids on Serbia lasted seventy-eight days and were the first international conflict in Europe since 1945 and it was also the first war in which not a single soldier on the victorious side was killed, and the military strategists said that it was a good omen for the future and that in future nobody would GOOD OMEN FOR THE FUTURE die in wars apart from enemies.

Psychiatrists said that in many people the First World War provoked traumas that had been previously hidden in the unconscious, and in the 1920s and 1930s the people started to be neurotic because they were not adapted to their inner or outer state, and in Europe in the 1960s, 25% of women and 15% of men were neurotic, and journalists called it the disease of the century. And in the 1970s the number of people suffering from depression also started to rise, and at the end of the century every fifth citizen of Europe was depressed.

Sociologists said that neurosis and depression mirrored the

cultural transformation of Western society in the twentieth century. And neurosis mirrored a society dominated by discipline and hierarchy and social taboos and that it was a pathological expression of a sense of guilt. And depression was a pathological expression of a feeling of helplessness and an awareness of emptiness. And people were originally neurotic because they would have liked to do forbidden things, but they could not because they were taboo, and when they violated the taboo they felt guilty. And later, when almost everything was permitted, they started to be depressed because they did not know what they
would like to have done, and they were transformed into new pathological subjects and psychiatrists said that the pathological subject had been totally transformed during that period. And sociologists said that depression was a compensation for a world in which individual freedom no longer represented an ideal that we must painfully struggle toward, but a barrier that we must painfully surmount. And neurosis was anxiety over the violation of taboos and depression was anxiety at the burden of freedom. And some people wanted to find some meaning in everything and suffered existential frustration. And psychologists said that looking for meaning in life was the result of a need to drive emptiness and death out of it and that it allowed one to live more intensely. And at the end of the 1980s, the World Health Organization issued a declaration that depression was the most widespread pathology in the Western world. But meanwhile new social prohibitions started to penetrate Europe from the United States, such as that one should not smoke or use salt or tell jokes about homosexuals or lead an indolent existence, etc. And on the contrary, lots of things were now permitted that were previously prohibited. And some people were neurotic and others depressed and yet

others were neurotic and depressed at the same time and they used psychotropic drugs and psychoanalysts said that people abused psychotropic drugs and did not attend psychoanalysis often enough. And that drugs simply shifted traumas deeper into the unconscious, but the only way to cure people was by verbalization of anxiety and rediscovering one's self-awareness. VERBALIZATI OF ANXIETY

In the Golden Age people were racists, but they did not know it yet, and they were curious about Negroes and Papuans, etc., and zoological gardens in big cities organized ethnographic spectacles, with savages sitting in front of bamboo huts with skins around their loins and making various things, and people went to watch how the Papuans and Ashanti and Zulus lived and threw them sweets and sugar cubes. Ethnographic spectacles enjoyed great success because people wanted to know how people lived elsewhere in the world, and at the World Exhibition in Paris in 1900 the advanced countries exhibited not only technical innovations and new art and new architecture but also examples of the aboriginal populations of their colonies—Nubians and Dahomeyans and Caribbeans and Malays and Kanaks. The Kanaks sat at the exhibition in front KANAKS SAT IN FRONT OF of bamboo huts with skins around their loins and ground HUTS stone clubs with flints, even though they had never before held a flint or a stone axe in their hands because they were junior clerks in the colonial administration recruited by the French government in the interest of the state. And when the World Exhibition ended, the Colonial Museum sent them on a tour of Belgium and Germany and Denmark, and the Kanaks wrote letters to the Director of the Colonial Museum asking when they would be allowed to return home and take up their duties but they never received any reply and one day all the Kanaks escaped from the railroad car they were being

taken around Germany in and they returned to France and
secretly boarded a boat that they heard was bound for New
Caledonia, but the boat was actually sailing to Lebanon. And
when the seamen found the stowaways and discovered they
THE SEAMEN
WERE PROUD were the Kanaks from the World Exhibition they were proud
that they had chosen their particular boat and they brought
them food and did not want to let them work and they asked
how many stone axes were manufactured in New Caledonia
per year. After the First World War, ethnographic spectacles
gradually became fewer, because 1,700,000 Zulus, etc., fought
during the war in the ranks of the Allied forces and people
became used to them and were not so curious.

Young people said that racism was a result of the old world and
that it was necessary to rethink the world, and televisions and
refrigerators were less important than love and happiness. And
they did not want their parents to tell them what they had to
YOUNG PEOPLE
WANTED SEXUAL
INTERCOURSE study and to forbid them to smoke and have sexual intercourse
and wear long hair, etc. And in 1968 there were student riots
in Western Europe and students erected barricades and went
round the factories persuading the workers that society had to
be changed from the foundations and they wrote on the walls
BLUE WILL REMAIN GRAY UNTIL IT HAS BEEN REINVENTED and
BE REALISTIC DEMAND THE IMPOSSIBLE and NO FORBIDDING
ALLOWED and POWER TO THE IMAGINATION and they occupied the lecture halls and theaters and smoked and had sexual
intercourse in various ways and discussed politics. The 1960s
represented an important watershed in the history of Western
society because material prosperity prevailed and women had
access to contraception and young people became an important component of public opinion and in time older citizens
started to engage in sports also and dress in young fashions
and have sexual intercourse in various ways and voice novel

and radical ideas and when someone was not young in spirit RADICAL IDEA
at least they belonged to the old world. And sociologists said
that bourgeois society was extinct and had been replaced by a
new form of society that they called adolescent and they said
that it indicated a radical change in the evolution of Western
society and that it was necessary to reflect on this. And some
philosophers said that the cult of youth was one of the silliest
things in the history of the human intellect and it was indica-
tive that it was invented by the Fascists and Communists, and
democratic societies were foolish enough to borrow the cult of
youth from the Fascists and Communists, but others said that
it was all right, that youth was possibly silly but it was dynamic YOUTH WAS
DYNAMIC
and that was positive. Sociologists said that being positive was
a new value in Western civilization and it had replaced traditional humanist values that were no longer appropriate to the
state of society. Being positive meant that people would look
forward to the future with confidence and take part in sports
and live healthily and harmoniously and visit the doctor regularly and live to an advanced age and work hard in order to
enjoy their retirement and wear young fashions. And no one
wanted to be poor anymore and everyone wanted to have a
refrigerator and a cordless telephone and a dog and a cat and
a tortoise and a vibrator and take part in sports and attend
psychoanalysis. Catholic philosophers said it was the fault of
Protestants because they emphasized the importance of material success and GOD HELPS THOSE WHO HELPS THEMSELVES,
whereas the Catholics believed more in WHOM GOD LOVETH
HE CHASTISETH. Protestant philosophers, on the other hand,
said the decline of the Catholic Church proved it was unable
to move with the times, and that mentalities evolved, and pas- MENTALITIES
EVOLVED
tors could marry and satisfy themselves sexually and so better
propagate Christian ideas in a society dominated by nihilism.
And people in cities got themselves dogs and cats and tortoises

and guinea pigs for their homes, because dumb animals were faithful friends even in an alienated world. And dogs and cats had their own hairdressers and beauty salons and fitness centers and convalescent homes and morgues and cemeteries, etc. And American soldiers returning from the Vietnam War joined together to build a memorial to the 4,100 American dogs who fell in Vietnam for freedom and democracy. And in the developed countries farms were set up that were known as countryside museums or countryside corners and city people would visit them to see what a horse or a cow or a hen looked like because farm animals had gradually disappeared from cities. And other animals became scarce too, such as badgers and owls and tree frogs and butterflies and beetles on footpaths, and ecologists said that it was the fault of environmental pollution and pesticides and exhaust gases, etc. And some ecologists used to carry out night raids on medical and pharmaceutical research facilities where tests were carried out on animals, and they released monkeys and rabbits and hamsters and dogs and snakes and frogs, etc. And more and more people thought that it was necessary to protect animals and they set up societies for the protection of animals and sometimes they dressed up as bears or falcons and demonstrated in city streets against hunters and against bullfights and against scientific experiments on animals and said it was inhumane to kill animals. Some of them were vegetarians and ate carrots, etc. Hunters said they hunted animals in order to maintain tradition, that traditions were being lost and that traditions were important in the modern world. And every year some hunter killed another hunter instead of a wild boar by mistake and the other hunters joined together and bought his widow a new washing machine or something similarly useful for the home.

*

In the Golden Age, there were still goats and hens, etc., living in the cities and the men smoked cheroots and stroked their whiskers and electric street cars ran through the streets, as well as horse cabs and barouches and horse-drawn buses. Horses were also used in cities to transport goods because trucks scarcely existed, as well as used by the army and the police. Many horses died in the First World War, particularly on the Eastern Front, where the Russian, German, and Austrian cavalries fought, and in 1926, German spies penetrated the stables of the Romanian army and put glander germs in the forage and 3,055 Romanian horses died. On the Western Front horses were mainly used for reconnaissance duty and transporting artillery and machine guns and food and planks for building trenches, and mounted regiments were kept on permanent alert because the generals hoped that as soon as the infantry broke through the enemy line and put the machine-gun emplacements out of action, the cavalry would win the day by a bold encirclement of the enemy, and in 1915 the French invented special gas masks for horses. After the war horses became scarcer in the cities and the army and most of the city stables were closed down or rebuilt as kindergartens, because the architecture of the stables suited the needs of kindergartens. During the Second World War, most armies reduced the numbers of horses, apart from the Red Army that kept eight hundred thousand horses on alert and waited for the Germans to run out of gasoline or get stuck in the mud. In Germany and other European countries at that time most sta- bles had been shut down by then or put to other uses, and in the Birkenau concentration camp the stables were also used as accommodation and one stable would house either 52 horses or 1,000 to 1,200 prisoners.

*

MORAL CRISIS Protecting traditions and the return to nature were important in the twentieth century because they helped confront the moral crises that had been frequent phenomena ever since people had had locomotives and steamships and factories and could no longer live in harmony, and the world was full of violence and poverty and injustice. And in 1906, there came together a group of young German and Austrian Anarchists who wanted to seek real life beneath the veneer of civilization and they moved to Switzerland and set up a commune there that they called MONTE VERITÀ, and there they promoted naturism and vegetarianism and natural harmony, and they wore their hair long and danced around camp fires and preached ideas. And gradually a movement came into being that was joined by young people from various countries. And they preached a new absolute art in harmony with nature and said that art was not a matter of aesthetics but of biology, and that the most absolute of the arts was dance because it was the first, and dance was capable of inspiring the creation of a new social order, and in the 1930s most of them joined the Nazis because the Nazis preached natural harmony and

COALESCENCE WITH THE EARTH the coalescence of the individual with the Earth, and they agitated against the Jews, on the grounds that they disliked nature and wanted to soil the human mind and uproot from it what enabled people to live in harmony. And one of the commune's members became a well-known choreographer in Nazi Germany and devised gestural dance for the German workers in order to increase productivity in the arms factories. And in 1917, an Italian soldier wrote in a letter to his sister I FEEL MORE AND MORE POSITIVE EVERY DAY. And in 1930, a French doctor announced the beginning of a new age that would transpire under the sign of Aquarius, which would give birth to a new human being and usher in a world without war and violence. And in 1921 a Scottish teacher set up an experimental school in Germany in which he wanted to try out new, revolutionary, and anti-authoritarian methods, and he said that teaching should be replaced by debating about various interesting subjects because traditional teaching was essentially undemocratic and encouraged aggression in pupils. The school was intended for pupils from five to sixteen, and if they did not feel like debating they could stay at home or go for a bicycle ride or build a secret hideout with their pals, and that was what was revolutionary. And more and more people believed that mankind was entering a new era that they called the NEW AGE, and which was supposed to start the moment the sun entered the constellation of Aquarius, and it was supposed to last 2,160 years, during which the left and right hemispheres of the brain would merge and mankind would undergo a mutation and a new spirituality would be born. The New Age was supposed to be harmonious and spiritual and interactive and no one was supposed to oppress anyone else anymore, because mankind was supposed to achieve a new level of cognition and all people were supposed to be spiritually and ecologically aware. People who believed in the New Age said that Aquarius aptly symbolized the change that would occur, because people thirsted after something new and Aquarius would quench that thirst. And the old world was supposed to be materialistic and mechanistic and analytical, and the analytical method fragmented the reality of things and the reality of things was supposed to be assessed synthetically. And they said that Western culture taught people to count the trees in the forest, but nobody saw the forest. People who believed in the New Age wanted to return to spiritual roots of human community and coalesce with cosmic energy, and they concluded that it was necessary to reassess young people's

PEOPLE THIRSTED AFTER SOMETHING NEW

COALESCE WITH ENERGY

education because the New Age could not find full expression while people continued to think in old ways, and they said that most important of all was harmony because it allowed the cerebral hemispheres to communicate freely and communication between the cerebral hemispheres would in turn enable all people to attain the other shore within themselves.

And in 1950, the Pope declared that the theory of evolution, according to which people come from apes and oysters and quarks, etc., was in no way in contradiction with the belief in man and the mission he received from God, and although the mortal frame may have arisen from some pre-existent living matter, the soul was created by God. And He created it from the very beginning, at the moment when the human body achieved its final form. And another Pope declared in 1996 that the theory of evolution was most likely valid but it did not explain the metaphysical, and that was the origin of religion. And he said that science might possibly answer the

OW AND WHY
MAN CAME
INTO BEING

question of how man came into being and the Bible would answer the question why he was created. And it would enable understanding of the contradiction between the physical continuity of the animal species and the ontological discontinuity caused by the arrival of man. People who did not believe in God or the New Age, or aliens, or spiritual elements, etc., said that man originated by sheer chance and that the world was

NATURE WAS
PERVERTED

absurd and not even nature could be trusted because it was perverted and it was crazy trying to find any meaning in it. And other people, who believed in God and the creation of the Earth, said that the theory of evolution was an attempt by Satan to defile man and the Pope was the Devil's lackey, and in 1930, one Baptist pastor manufactured a human footprint one hundred and eighty million years old to prove that man was as old as the dinosaur. Evolutionists said it was scandalous and the creationists said that it was scandalous to claim that man originated from monkeys, and the theory of evolution was an ideological trick and took away from man his most intrinsic quality, self-awareness, the will to self-perfection and work, etc. Evolutionists said that self-awareness and the will to self-perfection could be found in animals, and the Communists said that man was actually an ape who started to work, but some evolutionists did not agree and said that nature had meaning in itself even without work. Some evolutionists, on the other hand, said that work was important and social science was subject to the same laws and mechanisms as biology, and that lavish human care and social welfare, etc., encouraged indolence and impeded the evolution of mankind.

MAN WAS ACTUALLY AN APE

The Communists said that God did not exist and that only matter existed and that it was necessary to build a new world, ruled by justice for all those who put their shoulders to the wheel, and nobody would envy anybody else anymore, because everyone would have everything and no one would have anything that everyone else did not have. But before the new world came into being, the old world must be torn up by the roots and people must learn new thinking, because without new thinking the new world could not happen. And they said that everyone had to decide whether they wanted to stand on the side of progress, because otherwise they would be swept away by the hurricane of history. Communists maintained that the October Revolution had actually brought history to an end, because Communism was the fulfillment of the historical meaning of the human community, and that it was only a matter of time before Communism would be victorious throughout the world and history would no longer have any

A NEW WORLD

PEOPLE MUST LEARN NEW THINKING

reason to continue. And they said that Communism was not a political system but a historical category, and for those who did not grasp this and thought in old ways, such as traitors and egoists and the envious and subversives and alcoholics, etc., they invented a special place that they called the trash can of history, because until Communism became victorious throughout the world it was necessary to know who did not belong to history. Historians later said that Communism revealed a new danger for human civilization, namely, the disappearance of historical memory, and that formerly various dictatorships censored memory in libraries and museums, etc.

ANNIHILATION OF MEMORY

And they said that Communists had extended the annihilation of memory to all spheres of public and non-public life and had elevated it to a legal principle, and that was original. And in 1917, the Communists devised revolutionary tribunals that tried traitors and subversives and were capable of passing as many as three hundred and fifty death sentences in a single afternoon, which would not have been possible in a court that thought in the old way, and at the same time they introduced new and more modern methods of torture that were capable of obtaining confessions from traitors and subversives, as well as the addresses of other traitors and subversives. Among the best known tortures were THE EAR and THE SWALLOW and THE FLOAT and THE MANICURE and THE BABY ELEPHANT, which consisted in tying a subversive to a chair or a table and putting a gas mask on his head but without oxygen, and meanwhile the Communists beat the subversive with sticks and the subversive breathed more and more intermittently and soon fainted and the Communists took off the mask and revived him and demanded his confession and addresses. What was also original was that, instead of simply denying some historical event, the Communists would leave it in history but completely reinvent it. And when subversives refused to answer questions, the Communists threw them to specially trained dogs that were known as NUMBER ONE, NUMBER TWO, NUMBER THREE, etc., because in the new society everything had a number. And the photographs of various celebrations and congresses and important historical events would progressively be retouched to remove those Communists who in the meantime had perpetrated treason or conspiracy or a bourgeois life concept or wrong thinking, and photographs that originally showed eight Communists, for instance, eventually showed only two or three. The historical commissions paid close attention to photographs because when people stopped believing what was written they continued for a while to believe photographs, and the Communists concluded that it was necessary to adapt photographs to the march of history in the same way that new locomotives were adapted to the march of history, etc. And in 1919 they devised special psychiatric clinics for subversives and madmen because they concluded that whoever was against the revolution was either a subversive or a madman. And they sent the subversives to concentration camps and the madmen to lunatic asylums, where they gave them a special therapy that was called brainwashing. It was necessary to wash diseased brains, so that nothing old remained in them and they would be ready to receive new ideas.

PEOPLE
BELIEVED
PHOTOGRAPHS

NEW IDEAS

At the end of the century people in democratic countries started to have the feeling that democracy and the consumer society also led in a way to the extinction of memory and said that excess information was just as dangerous as Communist censorship and that people were cut off from their traditions and roots, etc., and that consumer society was inevitably heading toward oblivion because it was hedonistic. And that in the

EXTINCTION
OF MEMORY

long term excess information was even more dangerous than Communist censorship, because it didn't provoke a reaction and the will to resist, but instead weariness and resignation. And that democratic regimes led to the disappearance of all cultural and historical references and the dictatorship of uniformity. But other people pointed out that memory was actually an interaction between preserving and interrupting some event and that it was by nature selective, and if it were not it would not be memory but a mental disorder. And other people, for their part, said that memory was not constitutive in Western civilization, and in that respect it differed from other civilizations, and what was more important than memory in Western civilization were universal principles and the general will, which enabled it to switch from heteronomy to autonomy, and that democracy was not a matter of memory, tradition, etc., but of a contract between the community and the individual, which in itself lacked any historical or anthropological value, but enabled the administration and regulation of social institutions. What was peculiar to Western society was the principle of the avant-garde, which referred to the future just as well in art as in science and politics, and the role of memory in Western society probably corresponded most closely to the concept of memory in computers. Programmers distinguished between two types of memory, ROM and RAM, but most people, when they talked about memory in computers, had in mind RAM, RANDOM ACCESS MEMORY, and the people who thought that democracy and the consumer society contributed to the extinction of memory said that it was a portent of a world without memory in which everything would be random.

Young people considered that it was necessary to return to the roots of wisdom and that the industrial society and compulsory schooling had changed people's relationship to true knowledge. And they said that what was previously known by every child was now known only by a handful of experts, and children previously knew various herbs and could set traps for rabbits and weave balls out of fresh grass and roll cigarettes out of strawberry leaves and then wash their mouths out with nettle broth so as not to be scolded at home. Older people, on the other hand, said that what was previously known by only a handful of experts was now known by every child, such as square roots, etc. But young people believed that square roots were good for nothing, and they traveled to India and Nepal to discover Eastern wisdom, and they said that Christian morality enslaved people and that people in Europe knew only how to count trees whereas Indians could see the forest. And they did not want to live in a world of violence and poverty and environmental pollution and they went off to uninhabited areas of America or Scotland or France and set up communes there and smoked hashish and marijuana and had sexual intercourse and sang songs and taught their children how to live in harmony with nature and they upheld traditions and beat on hand drums and danced around camp fires and preached ideas. In the Communist countries, none of that was allowed and everyone had to learn the same things and people weren't free to travel. In the Communist countries being progressive meant that everyone worked for the good of the working people and most important of all was the working class because the working people had natural authority in society, and everyone wanted to be of working-class origin. In the democratic countries, being progressive tended to mean that it would be better if no authority existed at all and people did exactly what they set their hearts on, but they would still behave responsibly because everybody would be open-minded and respect

LIVE IN
HARMONY
WITH NATURE

one another. In the Communist countries, progressive writers wrote novels with working-class settings in order to show that being a worker was the best thing that could befall an open-minded person, or wrote about people who, at first, looked on the working class with disdain but then realized that among

A JOYFUL
RMENT AMONG
WORKERS

the workers was the germ of a joyful ferment, and they wanted to become workers or at least members of the working intelligentsia in order to assist the workers with new and bold ideas. In the democratic countries, on the other hand, progressive writers wrote about open-minded people who rebelled against authority and the Establishment and wanted to remain free even at the cost of being in conflict with society. And new art associations were set up in which young writers tried out new approaches to writing and experimental methods in order to express that the world was absurd.

At the end of the century, men smoked a third more than women and they also drove cars more often and the Americans and Germans had the most cars per capita, and the Greeks,

VOMEN LIVED
LONGER

for their part, smoked most of all. Women lived longer than men and committed fewer suicides and spoke on average a third more words per day and people in cities rode bicycles and took part in sports and went for morning jogs along the streets to refresh their lungs. Morning jogging was invented by the Americans who bought shiny shorts and air-sole shoes so as not to put their backs out of joint, and in 1985 one hundred and thirty-five Americans got heart attacks from jogging. People at the end of the century wanted to stay young and dynamic, but at the same time wanted to be politically and sexually correct too, and that meant they would not seduce women or smile at them lewdly, etc., or tell jokes about Jews and Germans and homosexuals. And some women sued their superiors for saying things with erotic connotations or for offering to drive them home with an immoral expression on their face, and in 1997, one American lawyer had to pay four million dollars in damages to his secretary for dropping chocolates into her cleavage. And in 1998, some Americans wanted to depose their President, who was having improper relations with an intern and had fondled her breasts and stuck a Cuban cigar into her vagina, and she had performed fellatio on him, such as when he was on the telephone to the Secretary of Defense, etc., and meanwhile the Americans bombed Iraq, and the Iraqis said that the Americans wanted to distract attention from the improper sexual behavior of their President. The Europeans wanted to be politically correct too, but rather less so sexually, because there was a great cultural tradition of seducing women, particularly in the Latin countries, whereas America tended to be puritanical. The average age of citizens in the democratic countries was higher than in the Communist countries, because people visited doctors more often and they ate fresh vegetables, etc., but on the other hand, people in the Communist countries smoked more because they did not see the point of living healthily and living to a ripe old age, and the lowest average age was in the developing countries that were known as the Third World countries. In the advanced countries people at the end of the century lived an average of 78 years and the people with the shortest lifespan were the citizens of Sierra Leone, who lived an average of 41 years. And the sociologists said that according to various criteria people enjoyed the best standard of living in Canada and France. And the United States was in 18th place and Sierra Leone was in 187th place. People in cities lived longer than people in the country and spoke five times more words on average. And doctors said that if people led healthy lifestyles and received optimal medical attention,

AMERICANS WANTED TO DEPOSE THEIR PRESIDENT

BEST STANDARD OF LIVING IN CANADA

they could live as many as 110 or 130 years, and some people
thought that one day mankind would become virtually immortal, and the ideal society would be created when people would
only die from unforeseeable accidents or suicide. Psychologists
said that if people wanted to live to a great age, they must
not dwell on the past but look to the future, because dwelling
on the past was unproductive from the point of view of lon-

gevity, whereas the future was full of tension and excitement
and unknown possibilities and people could imagine what the
world would be like in twenty or fifty years' time, and psychiatrists said that individual memories did not correspond
to reality anyway and manipulation of objective reality was a
defense mechanism of the human mind, and if people did not
have the possibility to manipulate the past they would die a lot
sooner. During the First World War, the average age in various
countries dropped by as much as 10 or 12 years, but in the
working-class strata, in contrast, the average age rose because
there was no unemployment and the working men and women
used to see the factory doctor and receive canteen vouchers in
order to assist more effectively the final victory. And lots of
people called for euthanasia to be legalized in hospitals and
certain laboratories offered to freeze peoples' bodies after they
died and they would be left in a freezer until the day when it
was discovered how to make people immortal or until it would
be possible to clone humans, because so far it was only allowed
to clone tunicates and invertebrates and water fleas and frogs
and sheep and cows, etc. Cloning was a technique that enabled
the creation of genetic copies of living organisms from a cell
and it was one of the ways to achieve immortality.

The First World War was also known as THE WAR TO END
ALL WARS. At the beginning of the war this was believed as

such everywhere because everyone believed they would win it
and there would be no need for further wars, as world peace WORLD PEACE
WOULD PREVA
would prevail. After the war it was only described as such in
those countries that were victorious, because people in those
countries believed there would be no more need for further
wars, but in the countries that lost, people did not altogether
think so. The First World War was chiefly won by the French
and British and lost chiefly by the Germans, while the Second
World War was won by the Americans and Russians and lost
chiefly by the Germans, and the war that occurred later and
which was called Cold because no direct military conflict took
place during it between the democratic and Communist countries, and instead proxy wars were fought in third countries,
was won by the Americans and lost chiefly by the Russians.
And some historians said that war was a natural extension of
political action, while others disagreed and said that on the
contrary, political action was a continuation of war and anyway war never ended but was simply transformed and assumed WAR NEVER
ENDED
a different form. And in 1989, Communism collapsed in
Europe and lots of people believed that democracy had finally
triumphed because it had vanquished two of the most mur-
derous regimes in human history, Nazism and Communism.
And they said it was a good opportunity to establish a new
world order. And it was said that Communism had caused
the death of ninety to one hundred million people, but the
former Communists said that for one thing it may not have
been entirely true, or maybe it was, but it did not really count
because the Communists had meant well. And the historians
said that Communism was too recent a historical phenomenon for it to be treated as a subject for research, but that
in time Communism would become a subject for historical
research and people would approach it differently and more

objectively. Before the fall of Communism, the Soviet Union and the countries of Eastern Europe were called the EASTERN GLACIER, because life in those countries was rigid as if frozen stiff, and in 1989 lots of people in Western Europe thought that the eastern countries should join the European Union as soon as possible, and they said that it would enrich the European identity. And people who looked forward to the twenty-first century and concluded that democracy had finally triumphed said that no totalitarian regimes would be able to exist in the future because totalitarianism operated on the principle of controlling and preventing information, which would no longer be possible since the Internet enabled people all over the world to communicate ideas and aspirations through space at the speed of lightning. And on the Solovki Islands, where large concentration camps were located, the Communists killed seagulls, terns, and auks to prevent the inmates from using them to send messages abroad and letting people find out what was happening in the concentration camps. And the prisoners in the concentration camps along the rivers Irtysh and Ob, who worked as lumberjacks, used to cut off a finger and tie it to one of the logs being floated down the rivers to the big cities in the hope that someone would notice the finger and realize that something bad was happening in the concentration camps. But in time it became plain that the people in the former Communist countries were not much interested in a European identity, and people in Eastern Europe had no confidence in European history. Some West European historians said that the people of Eastern Europe should be given time because they lacked an awareness of the dynamic of history because forty years of Communism had created a historyless void. But people from the Eastern European countries saw things differently and felt that they could provide the people

EUROPEAN IDENTITY

in Western Europe with lots of interesting experiences, and they felt abandoned and neglected. And psychoanalysts said that interrupted history was like interrupted coitus and orgasm was not the natural result of a spontaneous act but a way of overcoming frustration.

The Pentecostalists said that if people prayed and meditated a lot they could communicate with the Holy Spirit. Pentecostalists who communicated with the Holy Spirit spoke unknown and ancient languages, and said, for instance MOKRI HEROKHORA SHMETKHANA or KHARI SAHANAH ENTROPIKHO KESHEHER or EYEM ROWROU YEKILS IHT ABKRO CYM, and psycholinguists said that the Pentecostalists were reviving subconscious metalinguistic activity that was present in all human consciousness, and the sociolinguists said that it was a reaction to the discrediting of religious and political discourse, which in turn led to the discrediting of linguistic conventions and a loss of faith in the meaning of life and history and the need for radical change, which was expressed precisely by some new or unknown language. The need for a new language had been felt urgently ever since the industrial world had displaced traditional religious and social values, and some people suggested the invention of a universal language and said that when all people would speak the same language peace would prevail in the world and they invented such languages. During the First World War it sometimes happened that soldiers of national minorities or from regions where they spoke a dialect could not understand the language in which their commanding officers issued orders, and this led to various misunderstandings and strategic blunders. And one Breton soldier had a finger shot off by an enemy bullet in 1916 and his lieutenant sent him to the doctor, but the latter considered that it was unpatriotic to visit the doctor with such a petty injury and he handed the soldier over to a military court, who had him shot, because the interpreter who could have explained that the Breton soldier had been sent to the doctor by his commanding officer had been given a furlough in the meantime. At the turn of the twentieth century two hundred seventy-five universal languages were created of which the best known was Esperanto and the advocates of Esperanto said that Esperanto was like the telegraph but better. And in 1909, the Esperanto movement split into two wings because Esperanto was supported both by Christians and by anti-clericalists and Anarchists, and the Esperantist believers said that Esperanto could hasten the arrival of God's kingdom on Earth, and the anti-clericalists and Anarchists, on the other hand, said that Esperanto was an expression of social consciousness and the first step toward world revolution. Esperanto was initially keenly propagated by the Communists but in 1937 the Soviet government accused the Esperantists of cosmopolitanism and conspiracy against Soviet power, and five and a half thousand Esperantists were sentenced to death or to forced labor in concentration camps. And one Soviet linguist predicted that when Communism triumphed worldwide, the new world would manage without any language at all, because the symbiosis of all the workers would be such that it would be unnecessary to speak at all, and people would gradually forget all about language and they would communicate simply by contact and the power of their revolutionary thoughts.

People who looked forward to the twenty-first century said that the end of control over information meant the end of institutional power and was the final phase of democratization because in the future power would lie in the hands of

THE INTER-
PRETER HAD
BEEN GIVEN
FURLOUGH

ESPERANTIST
CONSPIRACY

individuals or citizens' interest groups. And this would eventually lead to the demise of traditional politics, and Internet users represented a new type of citizen, which they called a hypercitizen. The hypercitizen was the first supranational and totally free citizen in history and anyone could become one if they managed to stop thinking the old way and started to think differently, because in the coming world order, labor and capital and raw materials would no longer play any role. And parliamentary democracy would give way to hypercivic democracy and each hypercitizen would be equal to every other hypercitizen and everyone would live interactively. And every week one language and 35,000 hectares of forest expired on average. And 96% of the world's population spoke 240 languages, while 4% spoke 5,821 languages and 51 languages were spoken by only one person. And in 1996, the United Nations launched a program called UNIVERSAL NETWORK LANGUAGE, and many Anarchists studied Esperanto and in 1910 a handbook was published in Esperanto explaining how to assassinate political leaders. And in 1921 one French Anarchist called on the proletarian Esperantists to abandon the bourgeois Esperantist organization and rally to him and establish branches. And three hundred and seventy million people from 180 different countries had access to the Internet and could communicate with those who shared the same or similar interests, and connect, for example, with an association of Swiss mothers that gave advice on how to communicate with adolescent children, or with various citizens who were in spiritual communication with extraterrestrials and wanted to contact other citizens, or with Winnipeg schoolchildren who had found a dead weasel on a school trip and had written a composition on the life of weasels. And the Communists devised a special language that people called wooden, which was to be spoken in the new

society until people started to communicate through the power
of revolutionary ideas. Linguists said that the aim of wooden
language was to short-circuit communication in the public and
COGNITIVE   non-public spheres and so displace cognitive linguistic struc-
STRUCTURES
tures from human consciousness. The chief characteristic of
wooden language was that the words it used operated within
a complex system of connotations that referred to the machin-
ery of power. So words were deprived of their original meaning and given a meaning that became broader as the speaker
became more established in the political hierarchy. And when
one Communist met another, he would say, for instance HOW
HARVEST IN   IS THE HARVEST PROCEEDING IN YOUR DISTRICT? and the other
THE DISTRICT
would say WE HAVE RALLIED THE FARMERS TO THIS YEAR'S PLAN
or WE HAVE VIGOROUSLY SET ABOUT THE FINAL TASKS or THE
COMRADES HAVE SUBMITTED RATIONALIZATION PROPOSALS. In
the beginning wooden language was used mainly in relation
to work and political decisions of the State, but in time people learned to use it about everything—the weather, holidays,
TV programs or to explain that their wives had taken to drink
and did not want to attend the parents' association meeting
at school.

TELEGRAPH   In the First World War the telegraph was used mainly for
sending secret messages and intercepting the enemy's messages
and sending bogus messages to confuse the enemy. And in the
Second World War the English invented a computer to deci-
pher secret messages and in the sixties the Americans invented
the Internet because they were afraid that in some future world
war the Russians might be able to intercept information vital
for freedom and democracy. And three hundred and seventy
million people had access to the Internet and could communicate their ideas and yearnings freely and without inhibitions.

And some travel agencies offered via the Internet low-price virtual excursions to distant lands according to the personal wishes of each hypercitizen. And women could use the Internet to order sperm from anonymous donors and some laboratories offered sperm from men of a particularly high standard, such as astrophysicists, science graduates, basketball players, etc. Women could select the sperm according to one hundred and fifteen different criteria—nationality, origin, race, religion, educational attainment, hobbies and pastimes, occupation, height, weight, blood group, hair color, extent of body hair, size of testicles, etc., and could buy, for instance, the sperm of a thirty-six- year-old American biologist of Afghan origin who had black hair and blue eyes, or the sperm of a forty-two-year-old Baptist aircraft engineer from Kansas of Dutch-Ukrainian origin, or the sperm of a talented seventeen-year-old chess player of Chinese origin with small testicles. One sperm cost on average one thousand and fifty U.S. dollars including postage, and women could also order a recording of the donor's voice. The text of the recording was HELLO! THIS IS A REALLY LOVELY DAY, JUST MADE FOR WALKING IN THE COUNTRY. I HOPE YOU'LL BE SATISFIED WITH ME. And one woman who ordered the recording wanted to know if she could have a ten-percent discount because the sperm donor had a lisp.

SPERM FROM HIGH-STANDA MEN

COUNTRY WALKS

With the development of the industrial society, alcoholism also became widespread in Europe and America and many people believed that alcohol was the scourge of humanity and was an obstacle to the natural evolution of society. The Americans considered that alcoholism was a typical disease of European society and it was spread to America chiefly by the Irish and Italians. And some Americans demanded that measures be taken to deal with it, so that in the future the Irish

ALCOHOLISM

and Italians would not be admitted to the United States without previous psychiatric and social examination. And in 1919 the American government banned the sale and consumption of alcohol and in 1921 an immigrant quota was decreed that reduced the number of Irish and Italian immigrants by 85%. And in 1914, American psychiatrists urged that alcoholics be promptly sterilized in the interest of preserving a healthy, superior society. Americans were proud that in the United States it was possible to live a healthy, superior life, while in Europe people smoked and drank alcohol and breathed polluted air, and in 2000, the Americans repealed a law in Alabama that banned mixed marriages with Negroes. And American doctors recommended people breathe fresh air and take part in sports and ride bicycles, because it was a way of keeping fit. Bicycle riding was chiefly intended for American men, because the bicycle was somewhat unsuitable for women, and doctors said that for a woman a bicycle was above all a sexual partner and the rubbing of the saddle against the labia and clitoris WOMEN'S aroused women and incited them to perverted sexual prac-PERVERTED PRACTICES tices. In order to prevent perverted sexual practices in women a special saddle was once manufactured with a hole cut out in the middle, but it was rather uncomfortable. Bicycle riding spread widely in the eighties and nineties because people in the developed countries wanted to live healthily and take part in recreational activities, etc. And in the poor countries people rode bicycles too because they could not afford a motorcycle or car, and in Sierra Leone, 31% of adult citizens owned a bicycle. In the rich countries, where there were lots of cars, cyclists in cities wore oxygen masks to protect themselves from exhaust fumes that were dangerous for their health. Gases polluted the environment and released carbon dioxide into the atmosphere, which contributed to a phenomenon known as the greenhouse effect, which caused the temperature of the

Earth to rise. The greenhouse effect was originally necessary to allow life and intelligent creatures to originate on Earth, but ever since people had lived industrially, the concentration of gases in the atmosphere had increased and scientists said that it would lead to climatic instabilities. And in Germany the heads of companies asked their employees who owned old cars not to park in front of the entrance to the factory because it could give a bad impression, and in 1999 one commercial traveler was fired because he had an old and dirty car, but was lazy and parked right in front of the entrance and ignored reprimands. In Germany, people washed their cars nineteen times a year and in England fourteen times a year and in France ten times a year and in America twenty-eight times a year. Cars were more important in the Germanic and Anglo-Saxon countries than in the Latin ones, where the main thing was to be elegant and have a tasteful necktie and shoes, etc. And in 1939, the Nazis issued a law banning Jews from driving cars and when they caught a Jew driving a car they would send him to a concentration camp.

The Amish were against the Internet and war and consumer society and smoking and alcohol and they did not like electricity and used kerosene lamps for lighting and lived in settlements and drove to town in horse-drawn buggies and sold ecologically sound food and ecological coffee mills and ecological stoves and kerosene lamps and candles and rakes and whisks for whipping egg whites and they looked forward to the apocalypse, which would put an end to the Internet and wars, etc., and allow them to join the chosen and sit at the right hand of God. And the Jehovah's Witnesses said that smoking and alcohol soil the blood and they refused to eat black pudding and blood sausage and refused blood transfusions because the mixing of blood contradicted divine ordinances, just like the consumption of blood sausage or alcohol or extramarital

A COMMERCI
TRAVELER W/
FIRED

CONSUMPTIO
OF BLOOD
SAUSAGE

sex. And they refused to enlist in the army and said that they belonged to the Kingdom of God and worldly matters were no concern of theirs, and many of them died in the concentration camps in Germany and the Soviet Union because their attitude subverted the revolutionary ideal and propagated asocial and counterrevolutionary ideas in society. The Communists distinguished sixteen categories of asocial and counterrevolutionary elements and in 1919 they decreed obligatory quotas for each of the administrative zones of the Soviet Union. The first target figure gave the number of asocial and counterrevolutionary elements who were to be shot in a given district, the second figure the number of elements to be sent to concentration camps. The Soviet government also drafted a list of criteria governing the issuing of food ration coupons to citizens, which were known as class rations. The list initially comprised five groups of citizens, but later the Communists decided that the number of criteria did not fully reflect the social and political climate in society and they extended the list to thirty-three categories, and the first included Red Army soldiers and political commissars and in the last were the bourgeois canker and shirkers and hooligans and Orthodox priests and citizens of suspect nationality and other asocial elements who waited to be interned in concentration camps. And when the October Revolution broke out in 1917, some orthodox priests said that APOCALYPSE it was the start of the apocalypse and people should prepare for the end of the world. In the twentieth century apocalyptic sects proliferated and some of them organized mass suicides of their members and supporters, because it was the surest way of ensuring a future in the afterlife. And some sects built huge underground bunkers with their own electrical generators and sewage systems so that their members might have somewhere to shelter in the interim period that was to start after the end of the world and last until the Last Judgment. And in 1999 the Amish sold twelve times more coffee mills and candles and whisks for whipping egg whites, etc., than usual, because people were afraid that the MILLENNIUM BUG would deactivate domestic appliances and the supply of electricity. Sociologists thought that fear of a breakdown of electronic systems that would deactivate televisions and microwave ovens and auto-mated teller machines was the outcome of subconscious and suppressed millenarianism, and some people believed it would be a fatal moment in the history of Western civilization that would lead to chaos and social unrest, etc., and enable Western civilization to break free of the dictatorship of technology and enter a new age which would be harmonious and spiritual and mystical. And in some countries governments printed money to stockpile and in Canada the government organized practice evacuations of the population and in England and Denmark citizens stored reserves of sugar and flour in their bathtubs and in Finland the pharmacists sold out of all stocks of iodine, which was recommended in case of a nuclear disaster, and the Finns were scared that the MILLENNIUM BUG would deactivate all the security systems in the nuclear power stations in Russia. Sociologists said that the MILLENNIUM BUG would enter the logic of the social imaginary of the modern epoch and that in the twentieth century evil had assumed the form of something infinitesimal and people were no longer afraid of huge and complex things, such as locomotives, etc., but of atoms and viruses and genes and prions. And psychoanalysts said that the MILLENNIUM BUG actually played in the life of society the role of parricide, which would enable the new technological gener-ation to achieve independence and attain pleasure and delight.

Above the entrance to the Buchenwald concentration camp was the sign EVERYONE GETS WHAT HE DESERVES. The Buchenwald camp lay on the slopes of the Ettersberg Hill,

FATAL
MOMENT

SOCIAL
IMAGINARY

ETTERSBERG

which it was originally named after. The name Ettersberg was famous in Germany history because well-known writers and philosophers used to gather there in the eighteenth and nineteen centuries and go on walks and sit under an oak tree to discuss the meaning of European civilization. The Ettersberg concentration camp was opened in 1937, but a year later the cultural section of the Nazi Party in Weimar decided it was inappropriate to link the name of a concentration camp with the cultural legacy of the German people and requested the authorities to rename it. And from 1937 to 1945, 50,000 enemies of Nazi Germany died in Buchenwald and in the years 1945 to 1950, 7,000 enemies of the Soviet Union and the German Democratic Republic died in Buchenwald. The Buchenwald camp was a polyvalent concentration camp, for extermination and labor, and after their arrival the prisoners were tattooed on the forearm with a serial number. And in the first months of the war inmates received postcards with a pre-written text, which they were to send to their relatives. The postcards said THE ACCOMMODATION IS WONDERFUL, WE ARE WORKING HERE, WE RECEIVE DECENT TREATMENT AND ARE WELL LOOKED AFTER. When the relatives received the cards and pined for the sender they would report to the German authorities and ask to join their relatives in such-and-such a camp. And one Greek prisoner in Buchenwald sent the card to his father in Pyrgos and three months later the father came to visit him and at the railroad platform the son leaped on him and strangled him before the Germans managed to shoot him.

CARD TO PYRGOS

Scientific experiments also took place in the concentration camps. They mostly consisted of various methods of sterilization and castration and tests of resistance to pain, which were chiefly carried out on strong young prisoners who would have a piece of their foot cut off or the flesh stripped from their bones, etc., or various experiments with twins, which allowed new hypotheses to be formulated in the sphere of genetics, which were widely spoken about in specialist circles. And if someone who looked strikingly Jewish turned up among the prisoners, the Nazis cut of his head and stuffed it and sent it to German schools so that young people could recognize a Jew at first sight. Jews could be recognized by the fact that they had a hooked nose and villainous eyes and an evasive gaze and long bony fingers and they were often weak and sickly because nature had thrust them from her bosom. The twentieth century saw great advances in medicine and doctors invented penicillin and compulsory vaccination and blood transfusions and contraception and erection stimulants and women gave birth in maternity hospitals and received maternity leaves and people no longer died at home but in the hospital, surrounded by the best that modern medical care could provide. And Dutch scientists invented transgenic cows whose embryos were injected with human genes and when the cows grew up they gave human milk, which was recommended in preventive treatment of multiple sclerosis. But people who believed in the New Age said that modern medicine destroyed people's self-regulation capacity and instead of seeing the doctor and preventive treatment they recommended special auto-therapeutic methods, whereby patients modified their mental structures by positive thinking and mutated to a new physi- ological state in which they were no longer ill. And they said that real change in the world would result not from a scientific revolution or from some new religion or from political or economic reforms, but from individual spiritualization that would make people responsible and tolerant, and historical memory would be replaced by cosmic memory. And in Oregon the Americans legalized suicide under medical supervision and the Dutch legalized euthanasia. And nobody was absolutely poor anymore and everyone had a refrigerator and a television and paid holidays, etc., and scientists invented vinyl and Bakelite and polyethylene and microprocessors and inventors invented disposable products, such as disposable lighters, disposable pens, disposable razors, and disposable wrappings and bottles and tampons and diapers and cameras and hypodermic syringes, and sociologists said the society had entered a new cultural era of disposable objects, and the advanced countries became rich and unemployment grew, because the less people worked the richer they were. And advertising agencies devised original and witty advertisements and insurance companies declared BE REALISTIC ASK US THE IMPOSSIBLE and motor car manufacturers declared IMAGINATION HAS TAKEN POWER AT LAST and powder detergent manufacturers declared BLUE WILL REMAIN GRAY UNTIL IT'S REINVENTED, and in the democratic countries laws were passed preventing state presidents from holding office for more than two terms, which mostly lasted FRESH IDEAS four or five years, so as to ensure the supply of fresh and innovative ideas and a dynamic renewal of society. And philosophers said that the world had reached the civilization of copies, that everything was only a copy of copies of other copies, etc. And doctors invented a nonsexual way of creating children by placing spermatozoa and eggs in an incubator. The children born that way were known as test-tube babies and the first test-tube baby was born in 1978 and the doctor who invented the method proposed splitting the egg in the incubator, which SPARE TWINS would enable the production of spare twins. The first twin would then be placed in the mother's womb and the other would be frozen, and the twin from the freezer could later provide replacement organs for the twin from the womb when it grew up and its organs started to wear out.

*

Other inferior races were the Gypsies and Slavs. The Gypsies GYPSIES HAD DARK LOOK
had a dark look and limited intelligence potential and an
innate tendency to steal and murder. The Slavs also had limited intelligence potential and displayed an innate tendency
to sycophancy and servitude, but at the same time they were
lazy and incapable of concentrating on the simplest job. The
Nazis called the Slavs UNTERMENSCHEN, and that meant that
they were at a lower level of development than people, MEN-
SCHEN. And the children of long-skulled Slavs who could LONG-SKULLED SLAVS
prove German ancestry were to be taken away from them and
placed with German foster families. The Nazis estimated that
that there were roughly 12% long-skulled Slavs in Poland,
25% in Sub-Carpathian Ruthenia, 35% in Ukraine, and as
many as 50% in Bohemia. Gypsies and Jews were LEBENSUN-
WERT, which meant they were not life worthy, and half a million Gypsies and three million Jews died in the concentration
camps, and over two and a half million Jews died in the ghet-
toes and in raids and mass executions and on the way to concentration camps. And in 1941, special military units called
EINSATGRUPPEN were given the order to shoot as many Jews as
possible in the occupied territories, and within half a year they
had shot 800,000. And cakes of soap for German troops were
stamped with the letters RJF, and some historians said it was
short for REINES JUDENFETT, pure Jewish fat, and other historians said that it was short for INDUSTRIAL CENTER FOR FATS
AND CLEANING PRODUCTS. And in 1905, the German Institute
for the Gypsy Question published a ZIGEUNERBUCH, a Gypsy
Book, in which psychiatrists and anthropologists and biologists
explained why Gypsies were inferior and what danger they
might represent to society. And in 1922 the Germans devised
an anthropometric document for Gypsies, which replaced
the birth certificate, and in 1939 they decided to collect all

the Gypsies in concentration camps and move to the final solution, which was then known as global euthanasia. And in 1941 a long-skulled Pole invented a new universal language, Global German. And in 1936, the Nazis set up an institution called LEBENSBORN or FOUNTAIN OF LIFE, in which German women who wanted to offer a child to the fatherland were inseminated. The organization ran eight insemination institutes, fourteen maternity hospitals and six children's homes in which not only children of German women inseminated by selected members of the SCHUTZSTAFFEL, but also children of long-skulled Slavs were brought up, and over the entrance to the insemination institutes was the emblem of a well and the constellation of Ursa Minor with the large Pole-Star that symbolized Nordic blood. And in 1944, the administration of Birkenau concentration camp received an order to send all the remaining Gypsies to the gas chambers without delay and the camp administration decreed special night shifts that were known as ZIGEUNERNÄCHTE, Gypsy Nights. And meanwhile still more universal languages were created—Kosmolinguo, Latinulus, Mundial, Cosman, Komun, Neutral, Simplimo. And in 1985, the World Jewish Council issued a declaration that Jews fully sympathized with the Gypsy nation, but that the euthanasia of the Gypsies was not true genocide because it was based not on ethnicity but on social eugenics.

Historians later divided the political regimes of the twentieth century into three groups—totalitarian, authoritarian and democratic. The totalitarian regimes were Communism and Nazism, the authoritarian regimes were the Fascist and Fascist-inspired dictatorships that emerged after the First World War in Italy and Spain and Portugal and Greece and Poland and Romania and Hungary and Estonia and Latvia, etc. The

FOUNTAIN OF LIFE

Communists said that Fascism and Nazism were actually identical but most historians disagreed and said that Fascism was essentially universal and was capable of being implanted anywhere and immediately adapting to specific cultural and historical conditions, while Communism and Nazism were essentially inadaptable, because within them the reality of things is subject to ideology. And that was their totalitarian quality. And Fascism was adaptable and could be right-wing or left-wing and was directed at older citizens and revolutionary minded young people and promised the former to renew order and promised the latter to establish a new world in which everything would be eternally youthful. The eternally youthful world was something the Communists shared with the Fascists, but they had no intention of restoring order for older citizens. And young people looked toward the future and the wind ruffled the ears of corn and the sun rose on the horizon. And psychoanalysts said the fact that most Germans agreed with Nazi ideology was an expression of sexual frustration and the Germans were actually looking for a father, while Communism tended to be an expression of sadomasochism in its infantile phase.

The Communists proclaimed A HEALTHY MIND IS A HEALTHY BODY and maintained that psychoanalysis was an expression of the decay of bourgeois society, in which people had to compensate for the frustrations and feelings of inferiority that capitalism engendered in them. And in 1929 the Eugenics Research Institute in Leningrad proposed that particularly high-performing individuals be selected from the ranks of the Soviet workers and an insemination center be set up in which the selected individuals would inseminate Soviet women, and the Leningrad eugenicists calculated that a particularly high-performing worker was capable of supplying the Soviet people with as many as eleven hundred skilled workers and thereby reinforcing the healthy core of the future classless society. The Communists organized calisthenics each morning for factory and office workers and played them cheerful songs over the radio to help them work better, and they held parades and Spartakiads with allegorical floats and *tableaux vivants* and said it was a new art that was fed from the wellspring of the people. And the Nazis said that art was not an aesthetic but a biological issue, and that true art was the soul of the nation and belonged to all. And the Communists said that art should be as optimistic as the cocoon of a butterfly but also as determined as the people's march toward the future. And they propagated monumental art that could be seen from afar—statues or frescoes or enormous pictures, so that the ordinary people could take pleasure in art. The Nazis said that modern art was decadent and that the new artistic expression must be fed from the wellspring of the people, and the Communists suspected the artists of deliberately making decadent art in order to distinguish themselves more from ordinary people. And they said it was necessary to find a new artistic expression and new fresh ideas, but after a time they began to be suspicious of the fresh ideas because they might actually be an expression of bourgeois thinking that resisted true and revolutionary innovations under the pretext of modernism. And they started to be suspicious of people who wore moustaches or a hat or an extravagant coat or drew things in notebooks in cafes. And they said that art was to be an expression of the new life, optimistic and determined at one and the same time, and they organized calisthenics and played the workers songs over the radio.

ART BELONGED TO ALL

FRESH IDEAS

*

Concentration camps were invented by the Communists in 1918 in order to hasten the victory of the revolution and reinforce the dictatorship of the proletariat, and historians said that fifteen to twenty million people died in the Soviet concentration camps, and during the following thirty-five years one in seven adult citizens of the Soviet Union spent part of their life in them. And in 1916 there was a rising in Ireland. And in 1917 over two million soldiers deserted the Russian army in order to return home and not miss out on the distribution of the land and animals that had been promised them by the government that succeeded the Czarist regime. The Irish revolt was know as the Poets' Revolution because three quarters of the Irish revolutionary council were poets who wanted to establish an Irish republic and they counted on the English army's having insufficient resources to intervene effectively because most of the British troops were then fighting the Germans in France and Belgium. It was important to reinforce the dictatorship of the proletariat because the Bolsheviks had to fight not only against the bourgeoisie but also against the workers in the cities and peasants in the country who had different expectations of the revolution and were rebelling and striking and refusing to fulfill revolutionary tasks. And sixty-two rebels and one hundred and fifty English soldiers died in the Poets' Revolution. And the peasants who refused to fulfill revolutionary tasks had their harvest and cows and hens, etc., confiscated and the peasants who undertook hostile acts against the Soviet regime and went on stealing ears of corn from the collective-farm fields at night and refused to hand over their cow or sheep were sent to concentration camps or shot. Later the Communists decided that the best way to break the peasantry's hostile stance was to provoke a famine in the agricultural zones of the Ukraine, the North Caucasus, or Kazakhstan. And they diverted railroad

DICTATORSHI
OF THE
PROLETARIA

PEASANTS
REFUSED TO
FULFILL TASK

traffic and blocked the access routes and closed shops and banned markets, etc., and six million people died of hunger. And some people hid the corpses of their relatives and sold them on the black market or to their neighbors, and for the money they received they bought meat from other corpses, because they did not want to eat the flesh of those with whom they had possibly spent a pleasant time in the past. And the bones of the corpses were boiled for stock and the liver was used as a pie filling. And one peasant settled by a mass grave near the settlement of Bogoslovka and cooked himself meat from corpses, but the Communists found him and shot him as a warning to others. Originally there were two types of concentration camp, labor camps and special camps, and in the former a sense of politically conscious effort was instilled into alcoholics and hooligans and parasites and those who failed to fulfill the minimum number of shifts or left their workplace before making sure they had fulfilled their daily revolutionary target, while in the latter there labored disreputable and dangerous individuals, members of other political parties, workers caught
BOURGEOIS taking part in strikes, suspect civil servants, the bourgeois can-
CANKER ker, subversives and lunatics and Anarchists, landowners and potato thieves, and revolutionary commissars who had failed to send the required quota of counter-revolutionaries to the camps. And in 1922 the labor camps were abolished, leaving only the special ones, and everyone labored together for the good of all. And in 1923, two hooligans were also sent to the concentration camp at Murom after mocking workers on their way home from work, as well as a machinist who had come to work late three times in a row, and one night the machinist bludgeoned the two hooligans to death with a plank from his bunk for telling anti-Soviet jokes and the machinist was afraid that if he listened to anti-Soviet jokes someone would

denounce him and he would be shot. And after the Second World War all Russian prisoners of war returning home were PRISONERS OF WAR suspected of insufficient fighting spirit and individualistic tendencies and sent to concentration camps. The prisoners of war returning to the Soviet Union numbered 2,270,000 and on average, they spent ten years in the concentration camps, that is if they managed to survive diseases and epidemics. But the most common causes of death in the concentration camps were frostbite and gangrene of the legs, because people slept with their boots on as they were afraid of someone stealing them during the night.

Historians said that the mobilizations of 1914 were consistent with the mood of society in Germany, Austria, Serbia, France, Italy, etc., and that the First World War was possibly the first truly national and patriotic war in history. And when the soldiers marched through a town to the station, people PEOPLE SHOUTED SLOGANS all crowded into the street and shouted patriotic slogans and stuck carnations into the muzzles of the soldiers' rifles and a band played them rousing tunes. And in England, where in 1914 there was no compulsory military service, more than one and half million volunteers signed up, and they marched to the station and rejoiced that the war would arouse in them the virtues that modern industrial society had pushed into the background, such as love of the homeland and courage and self-sacrifice. But as the war continued and there were more and more mines and entrenchments and scabies and rats, the soldiers were less and less sure what they were actually fighting for and felt abandoned and unloved. And they used to shoot at the rats and make ashtrays for themselves and use a knife to carve into them such inscriptions as LONG LIVE THE 25th COMPANY, A SOUVENIR FROM THE WAR, GOOD HEALTH! and NEVER

AGAIN! In France and England there were lots of pacifists after the First World War and public opinion was peace-loving, and meanwhile the Germans were making uniforms and manufacturing tanks and airplanes. And in Spain a civil war broke out and the Fascists fought against the Communists and the Communists fought against the Anarchists to bolster the revolution, while the Anarchists wanted the revolution to be permanent and the Fascists wanted it to be national. And the pacifists said that peace was the supreme virtue, but the Nazis thought that the supreme virtue was victory and the grandeur of human destiny was the struggle between good and evil and the Communists considered that it was necessary to hasten the victory of Communism, and in Spain a civil war broke out and the Germans invaded Poland and Denmark and Norway and Holland and Belgium and France and the Russians invaded Poland and Estonia and Latvia and Lithuania and Finland and Romania, and so it started to be evident that the Second World War had begun.

GERMANS WERE MAKING UNIFORMS

Some historians preferred the Second World War to the First and said that the First World War was a national and patriotic war, while the Second was for the defense of civilization. And in the First World War people were fighting for narrow-minded concepts that were already outdated, whereas in the Second World War they were defending a humanist ideal. After the Second World War people did not become pacifists and instead tended to speculate about whether a Third World War would occur between the democratic and the Communist countries. And there were spies snooping around everywhere. And the ministries of information pondered on ways of assisting the final victory. And scientists invented new weapons and new poison gas and atom bombs and warheads and carriers

NARROW-MINDED CONCEPTS

and bombs with parachutes and electromagnetic perturbations and neutron radiation and macromolecular cytotoxicity. And new words and expressions were invented to describe the new scientific discoveries and inventions, as well as the new social phenomena and theories, THE THEORY OF RELATIVITY and BLACK HOLE and TELEVISION and YUGOSLAVIA and CRIMES AGAINST HUMANITY and RADIO and MODEM and DADAISM and SOCIOGENETICS and POSTMODERNISM and GENOCIDE and BIOETHICS and EUGENICS and TRANSGENOSIS and CUBISM and EXOBIOLOGY and NUCLEAR DISINTEGRATION and INTRAPERSONAL RELATIONS, etc.

<small>BLACK HOLE</small>

Some philosophers said that the order of the world corresponded to the mechanisms of a discourse which has both changing and given signs and that while the classification of the signs does not make much sense and everything is a game and chance and anarchy and process and deconstruction and intertextuality, etc., the sign itself is actually a vehicle of meaning although we do not know exactly what of. But other philosophers said that signs, which were the building blocks of discourse and the world, did not have any meaning and in the absence of meaning both the subject and reality itself ceased to exist and history was simply constant shapeless movement that expressed nothing, and everything was fiction and simulation. And the decline of humanism was logical because humanism had gotten itself into a blind alley precisely because it had achieved its aims and asserted its own values of freedom, individualism, pluralism, transparency, etc. And the humanists were now reaping what they had sown—an individualist and interactive and positive and translucid and operative world that expired in its own simulation and whose final solution was to substitute hyperreality for reality. And some mathematicians

<small>EVERYTHING WAS FICTION</small>

said that reality was an illusion and in fact it was a mathematical construct in the human brain that interpreted frequencies coming from some other dimension, one that transcended space and time, and the brain was a hologram reflecting the universe, which was also a hologram. And in 1993, an old lady who had once been a convinced Nazi willed her brain to a laboratory in Copenhagen so that the images stored in it might be shown to her grandsons and granddaughters because she had never been able to relate her life to them.

In 1907 a Frenchman crossed the English Channel in a powered aircraft and in 1910 a Peruvian flew over the Italian Alps in a powered aircraft and in 1911 the Italians used a powered aircraft in the war against Turkey and in 1914 aircraft designers figured out where to place machine guns so that aircraft could fire at each other and in 1915 they figured out how to drop bombs from aircraft, and in 1945 the Americans invented ATOM BOMB the atom bomb and dropped it on a city called Hiroshima. The aircraft was named ENOLA GAY and the pilot subsequently explained to journalists that he had named it after his Irish grandmother, because she had such a funny name. The explosion wiped out most buildings within a radius of three kilometers and a cloud of smoke formed in the sky, which started to be called a mushroom because it looked like one. A first-aid post was set up in the local school and the school children who survived the explosion picked maggots out of patients' wounds with chopsticks, and when patients died they carried them away to the crematorium on wheelbarrows. And in the following months more people died from illnesses they called atomic diseases, leukemia, asthenia, etc. People who survived the explosion and the atomic diseases scared other members of the population because they looked like lepers and behaved like madmen. Afterwards a lot of people thought it had been gratuitous brutality to drop an atom bomb at the very end of the war, but the military strategists said that if the Americans had not dropped it, someone else would have, because it had to be tried out at least once in real conditions in order to create a balance of terror as a guarantee against the outbreak of a third world war. And in 1944 the Americans invented a life-sized dummy called RUPERT. Rupert was dressed as a parachutist and stuffed with hand grenades and explosives and the Americans dropped him out of planes behind enemy lines and when the Germans or partisans saw Rupert landing they rushed over to him and when Rupert hit the ground he exploded and killed everyone standing around. And in 1918 the Germans invented a gun called BIG BERTHA that had a range of 128 kilometers and in 1944 they invented a guided missile called a VERGEL-TUNGSWAFFE that achieved a speed of 5,800 kilometers per hour and was intended to achieve Germany's final victory. And in 1947 the Americans invented a supersonic aircraft and in 1957 the Russians invented an artificial satellite and in 1961 they sent the first man into space, and in 1969 the Americans sent three astronauts to the Moon and when the first astronaut climbed down the ladder onto the Moon's surface he uttered the historical sentence THAT'S ONE SMALL STEP FOR MAN, ONE GIANT LEAP FOR MANKIND. The chief engineer of America's space program was a former colonel of the special units of the German army known as SCHUTZSTAFFELN, who had invented the VERGELTUNGSWAFFE guided missile in 1944. There was subsequent controversy over whether the astronaut had thought up the historical sentence on his own or whether it had been previously thought up for him by a public relations expert. The VERGELTUNGSWAFFE guided missile was manufactured at the Dora concentration camp, and 528 million television viewers

REAL
CONDITIONS

GERMANY'S
FINAL VICTORY

watched the live coverage of the landing on the Moon and politicians and public relations experts said that it was a major step toward worldwide communications and the achievement of higher-quality interpersonal relations.

And during the Second World War, physicists reappraised the theory of relativity and mathematicians invented the theory of information, which was innovative because it ignored the semantic field and conceived of information as something that was unrelated to meaning. And some mathematicians and astrophysicists said that information was one of the constitutive components of the universe and the organization of the universe was the result of the converse relationship between energy and information, on the one hand, and information and matter on the other. Philosophers said that information was a philosophical concept and it was the putting of being into form and there was always a trace of content, although of itself it had no meaning apart from the movement hidden within it, but which can also be expressed outside of form, and they posed the question of whether the absence of significance in information had any connection with the absence of meaning in history. Some mathematicians said that the Theory of Relativity had furnished the mathematical foundation for a new view of the world and the theory of information logically complemented it. The Nazis initially disagreed with the Theory of Relativity and said it was an aesthetic and intellectual offensive by the Jews, who sought to damage the German nation, and the Communists said that the Theory of Relativity had been invented by the bourgeoisie to prove that science as such was relative, and thereby impugn Communism, which stood on firm scientific foundations.

*

The First World War was national and patriotic and people believed strongly in patriotism and the national soul and war memorials and long after the Second World War, which was called the war of civilization, people still thought more in terms of nation than civilization, and every nation had its specific characteristics. And the English were pragmatic and Englishwomen had big feet and Italian women had big breasts and Italians were carefree and Germans were hygienically minded and had no sense of humor. And the Irish were permanently drunk and the Scots were good walkers and the French were arrogant and the Greeks had hang-ups and the Czechs were cowards and the Poles permanently drunk and the Italians boisterous and the Bulgarians backward and the Spanish cheerless and the Hungarians bigheaded. And sculptors and masons were glad they had lots of commissions. And the French had SAVOIR VIVRE and the English had a sense of FAIR PLAY. And on important occasions children stood guard at war memorials to show that the witness to war would remain forever and that people ought to give it thought. Anthropologists said that memorials were better at arousing reflection than museums or archives, because they appeal to memory rather than history, and memory is renewed whereas history removes the legitimacy of the living past by fixing it in time. And historians said that memorials helped classify society's memories and organize the collective memory and fight against oblivion in general and above all against specific oblivion, and that it was actually also a way of creating other forms of oblivion, and philosophers said that even oblivion could be structural. Memorials stood in various places—in public precincts, in the open air, at the roadside or on battlefields, and anthropologists said that in the twentieth century the placing of memorials in various places served to reorganize symbolic

NATION AND CIVILIZATIO

ORGANIZING COLLECTIVE MEMORY

space, and the organization of space was the basis of individual
and collective identity in society and was, at the same time,
a social institution and intellectual pattern and hence also a
first condition of all history. The people who stopped at the
memorial had the feeling of sharing slightly in the lives of
the soldiers and partisans and concentration-camp prisoners,
and also slightly in their deaths, and some historians said that
memorials were like shellfish on the seashore when the tide
ebbed along with memory, or like worms cut in half, in which
there still wriggled a remnant of life, which was no longer real
but symbolic. And one young Jewish woman survived the war
thanks to playing an aria from *The Merry Widow* on the violin
on the railroad platform at Struthof concentration camp. And
men and women had their hair shorn and they were handed
out tickets and told they would have to present them at the
ticket office of the baths. And in 1917, an Italian soldier wrote
in a letter to his sister I FEEL MORE AND MORE POSITIVE EVERY
DAY. And in the countries occupied by the Germans, people
after the war organized round-ups of collaborators and traitors, etc., and women who had slept with Germans had their
hair shorn, and one concentration-camp prisoner returned
home with a shaven head and went to a dance with his sister's
girlfriend, whose hair had been shaved off by local citizens
because she slept with the German occupation troops, and
they danced together with their heads against each other and
other people found it improper and almost in bad taste. And
the Spanish danced the flamenco and the Gypsies cast dark
glances and the Russians were arrogant and the Swedes pragmatic and the Jews devious and the French carefree and the
English bigheaded and the Portuguese backward. But with the
development of the consumer society and means of communication people's lifestyles in Europe gradually came to resemble

EBB OF
MEMORY

each other and some sociologists and historians believed that it was outmoded to think in terms of nation and said that the most characteristic feature of Western industrial society was cosmopolitanism and that there was actually no such thing as Germans or Romanians, Swedes, etc., that they were simply self-projections into social stereotypes and prejudices. But other sociologists disagreed with them and said that with the development of the consumer society and means of communication, people gradually lost most of their points of reference and that the national community had paradoxically become more important than ever. And stereotypes were essential for preserving collective and historical memory, without which Western society would lose its cultural unity, because unity could not but be heterogeneous. And collective memory was a compromise interaction between the past and the present and stereotypes and prejudices had the advantage of aging more slowly than history and technological innovations, etc., and that they represented the last and also most active sphere in which social identity was preserved. Ethnologists and anthropologists said that historicity can assume two forms, one of which was peculiar to societies that wanted to preserve their symbolic existence and the other to societies that tapped events and energy from history. And Western society traditionally fell into the second category but at the present time was possibly shifting to the first. And philosophers said that the acceleration of history that had occurred in the twentieth century resulted in an indifference toward time and the demise of historicity in its traditional form, and if another form of historicity was to emerge it was necessary to slow history down, and some of them demanded that the Declaration of Human Rights should include the right to human time. The idea of building war memorials lest soldiers be forgotten arose during the war, when

SELF-PROJECTIONS

SOCIAL IDENTITY

town mayors decided that the lists of fallen soldiers displayed outside town halls were too officious and uninspiring and not symbolic enough. After, the war memorials were built in the victorious and the defeated countries, and in the victorious countries they chiefly celebrated victory and sacrifice and in the defeated countries chiefly sacrifice and courage. And in 1989, an American political scientist invented a theory about the end of history, according to which history had actually come to an end, because modern science and new means of communication allowed people to live in prosperity, and universal prosperity was the guarantee of democracy and not the contrary as the Enlightenment philosophers and Humanists had once believed. And citizens were actually consumers and consumers were also citizens and all forms of society evolved toward liberal democracy and liberal democracy would in turn lead to the demise of all authoritarian forms of government and to political and economic freedom and equality and a new age in human history, but it would no longer be historical. But lots of people did not know the theory and continued to make history as if nothing had happened.

END OF
HISTORY

PATRIK OUŘEDNÍK was born in Prague, but emigrated to France in 1984, where he still lives. He is the author of over twenty books, including works of fiction, poetry, and essays. He is also the Czech translator of works by such writers as François Rabelais, Alfred Jarry, Raymond Queneau, Samuel Beckett, and Boris Vian. He has received a number of literary awards for his writing, including the Czech Literary Fund Award.

GERALD TURNER has translated numerous authors from Czechoslovakia, including Václav Havel, Ivan Klíma, and Ludvík Vaculík, among others. He received the U.S. PEN Translation Award in 2004.

Printed in the USA
CPSIA information can be obtained
at www.ICGtesting.com
JSHW080440190424
61487JS00005B/7

9 781628 975017